KNIFE EDGE

KNIFE EDGE

A Novel by Ralf Rothmann

TRANSLATED BY BREON MITCHELL

A NEW DIRECTIONS BOOK

© Suhrkamp Verlag Frankfurt am Main 1986
Copyright © 1992 by Breon Mitchell

Published by arrangement with Suhrkamp Verlag, Frankfurt
am Main
Manufactured in the United States of America
New Directions books are published on acid-free paper.
First published clothbound and as New Directions Paperbook 744
in 1991
Published simultaneously in Canada by Penguin Books Canada
Limited

Library of Congress Cataloging-in-Publication Data

Rothmann, Ralf.
   [Messers Schneide. English]
   Knife edge / Ralf Rothmann ; translated by Breon Mitchell.
     p.   cm.
   Translation of : Messers Schneide.
   ISBN 0–8112–1204–1. — ISBN 0–8112–1210–6 (pbk.)
   I. Title.
PT2678.O84M413   1992
833'.914—dc20   91–43449
                                      CIP

New Directions Books are published for James Laughlin
by New Directions Publishing Corporation.
80 Eighth Avenue, New York 10011

To look on is a crime.
All I know are feelings.
Nicolas Born

KNIFE EDGE

It rained that afternoon, wind lashed the muddy puddles, gulls from the nearby canal cried out beneath the dark gray sky. A bartender in a leather apron pushed a drunk out of a bar, fending him off with an upturned chair. In the flower shops the first asters had appeared, small black plastic pots on Styrofoam trays, mountains of grapes everywhere, bodies wrapped in loose woolens, scarcely a top button undone. Strollers disappeared, colors faded, over night, faces regained their old wrinkles. Days were darkening earlier, buildings stood out more blackly against the sky, neon signs glowed more peacefully. As if a consciousness had passed through all forms, tracing them with a new strength of thought, contours seemed more sharply etched.

*

Manfred Assen, who was driving a taxi part time, not wanting to write for a living, parked his car in Grunewaldstrasse and turned off the light. He was feeling sick, the way he used to feel when he was a kid and had pulled some stupid trick—like running away again from the teacher who beat him, or faking his parents' signature—and wound up sitting by the kitchen window waiting to be punished. His mother was still cleaning the bathroom, humming a tune, but in the shimmering glasses in the cabinet, on the chrome trim of the cold coal stove, in the gleam of the sparkling

1

clean sink, in the reflection of polished apples in the windowpanes, he saw only flashes of her coming rage. He watched the other children playing together contentedly in the yard, and even though one of them, climbing up a birch tree, imitated the howls he soon expected to hear and grinned broadly at the others, his playmates seemed to exist in a state of heavenly innocence from which he saw himself expelled for all time—without actually feeling guilty. He could hear his mother arranging bottles and lipstick tubes on the glass shelves; there was no way out of it. Or should he stick a piece of cardboard in the seat of his pants, like they kidded about in school. She'd notice it the moment she hit him, and just whale away harder. His playmates, having reached the end of the garden, jumped into the gravel pit, jackets billowing. In the afternoon sky, too far away, he saw the pale mouse hole of the moon. He smelled nail polish remover, and suddenly remembered how he once escaped a beating because his mother didn't want to ruin her freshly painted nails. But this time she was already standing in the kitchen, rummaging about in the drawer for a wooden spoon.

At the first blow Assen wet his pants a bit. Each cry was meant to soften his mother, but only enraged her more. When the wood finally splintered, she glanced quickly at what was left of the handle and then at him. With a cry that seemed enraged and desperate at the same time, she grabbed him by the hair and banged his head against the sink. A tooth broke. She released him abruptly and wiped the blood from the basin.

*

What tortured him about the power Iris had over him now was that she made no use of it, that she left him alone with his fear of it. He saw her bustling about her sister's house in Bacchereto, arranging things carefully for what was to come. She rode her Solex into the village to buy a small pot and a spark plug. She weatherproofed the windows for winter, scraped moss from the gutters, chopped wood, and when the ax got stuck she drove it in further with a brick. The local women were clearly on her side. They provided her with woolens and a thermometer for the bath water, showed her their wedding pictures, photos of children and grandchildren, and when she walked by, the men in front of the café looked aside and pulled at their ears. At night she would shove the kitchen table in front of the house, drink a little wine, and look down on the lights of Prato, a shimmering, shifting play of rays, like a song.

That she wished to bear this child, even against his will, compelled his respect. Up to now, he'd only thought of bearing something in the sense of bearing pain, the pain of battle or a fight; now she was bearing love, her feelings had taken on form. Her decision sounded to him as cold and final as a death certificate. He imagined himself trying to talk her out of it, saw her listening—and all the while she argued, or saw his point, or wept, her decision remained unshakable, firmly fixed in her eyes from the beginning of time. He could like it or lump it. And when, in his despair, he spoke of the desolate state of the world, of war, and cancer, and acid rain, she looked at him a long time wordlessly and said at last: That's a risk I'll have to take. She'd said "I," but he'd been thinking of the child. Touching her stomach tenderly, she walked away without looking back. He would fall in line soon enough.

(In the kitchen, beneath the woodpile by the stove, lived a mouse so big and black that everyone took it at first for something far more dangerous. Sometimes, paying no attention to the people sitting about, for no obvious reason at all, it would race in great zigzags across the flagstone floor, scrabbling madly as if driven by something far more terrifying than anyone present.)

She noticed him, Iris said later, because even though he usually came to the bars alone, he didn't have the nervous look or panic-stricken talkativeness of most single men, and didn't seem to be looking for a woman. She was attracted by the melancholy defiance in his face and by his eyes, in which she saw more than simply nightlife.

She sat next to him at the bar, drinking a beer, and after a period of silence asked him for a penny. He let her see he thought she was being silly, but gave her one mark. She shoved the coin back, clearly annoyed; she didn't need money she said—she needed a penny! He pulled one from his jacket pocket, she thanked him brusquely, looked around quickly, and lifted her skirt up a notch beneath the shadow of the bar's rim. A button on her garter had torn off, one strap was hanging limply; she wrapped the copper coin in the black fringe and fastened the loose clasp to it. Then she left.

*

At a party in Kreuzberg—his friend Lauter was flopped under a bed drinking from a flask—he saw her again. She stood near him, but tried to give her face a distant look. Talking only with other women, she strolled through the long halls, avoiding his eye so obviously that he felt she was watching him. In fact on one of the video screens installed everywhere he spotted her inspecting him on another screen. Finally she walked toward him, slowly, in black and white. Then—thrusting out her hand with shocking abruptness—she gave him back the penny, in full color. Around midnight she maneuvered Assen, who was stumbling drunk, into a small room containing a convertible sofa and two refrigerators stuffed with books. Beyond that he only recalled that her body left nothing to be desired. Perhaps that's why he thought no more about her. A few days later a stranger called.

He turned down an invitation to dinner, claiming he had work to do, he didn't want to get involved. Whatever you say, she replied. It sounded a little threatening, and she didn't hang up. But precisely because she gave him time to change his mind, he didn't. And then he remembered again the breathless intensity with which they had fallen upon each other, with no tender preliminaries, without a single kiss—as if each wanted to pass right through the other, to put the other one behind, once and for all.

*

The next day the central dispatcher sent him to a telephone booth on Akazienstrasse. Iris was wearing a black raincoat with yellow buttons and didn't smile when she saw him. She wanted to go to a bakery two blocks away, and since it was almost closing time, she told him to step on it. Assen switched on the meter. She asked him to wait outside the store, and knowing what he was probably thinking, left her coat and purse in the back seat. She bought a long baguette that got caught in the car door when she slammed it shut. She took a bite from what remained and called out her next destination with a full mouth, a Turkish vegetable stand on the next street. She offered him the baguette, there was lipstick on it, he shook his head. Next came a laundromat, a shoemaker, and a wineshop. The plastic bags slid across the seat whenever Assen turned a corner; a tomato rolled between the gas pedal and the brake and was squashed flat. He inspected Iris in the rearview mirror, seeing only the feigned unconsciousness of a woman who knows she's being watched. The shop lights flitted across her face, a drop of rain glittered in her lashes. At first glance she was disturbingly beautiful. Which meant the effect could only be diminished by each subsequent look, he told himself soothingly. He switched off the taxi meter, but that didn't make her any more talkative. The fact that she was doing the hunting, although she certainly wished in some sense to be taken as prey, impressed him too. He admired her cunning, the daring weakness that was an act of strength. Her vulnerable position would shame any predator, render his power harmless. When she smiled, he saw she was missing a tooth; an appealing gap way in the back. What wine would you like, she asked in front of the store. That depends on what you're cooking, he replied.

*

Her basement apartment was tiny, one room, a kitchen, and a bath; he didn't see many books. Still in her coat, Iris placed a pot on the stove and cut up the vegetables. Several photos on the wall showed her holding a baby, her sister's child she called in to him from the kitchen, although he hadn't asked. He offered to help, but when her brisk efficiency left him standing about awkwardly, he gave up and turned on the TV. After they ate, a dinner table was set in the film, then there was an explosion of some sort. What sort of poetry do you write, asked Iris, looking at the screen: love poems? What other kind are there? he said. When she turned off the television, he noticed she had a run in the heel of her stocking, stopped with a drop of nail polish.

Now the room was quiet except for the crackling of the television tube. Countless needles had been stuck into the wallpaper, casting countless shadows in the flickering candlelight, tiny sundials. Iris wanted to know if he thought she was too pushy. He waved her off with a yawn. She stood before him with her legs spread wide and her arms crossed on her chest. Did he feel flattered. Without really lifting his head, he looked up at her. I don't feel anything, he said, and her smile was a mild reproach, as if he'd better reconsider that. She took the wineglass from his hand, and they undressed quickly in separate corners of the room. Change

rattled to the floor. Transported to some other planet by
their sudden nakedness, Assen asked how much rent she
paid per month. He was so embarrassed by his question he
didn't hear the answer.

The wing of the corner building in which he lived was
empty, except for his room on the fourth floor. Once, young
painters, sculptors, and filmmakers had lived there. They'd
been thrown out on the street. I'm converting all the apartments to artists' studios, the landlord told him, back when
Assen was still on speaking terms with him. He was renovat-
ing the building himself, and slept there at night on an air
mattress, surrounded by cement sacks and tool boxes. He
kept his portable TV set under a plastic cover because of the
dust. During the day his curses echoed through the ducts of
the building, an indistinct baying. Whenever he banged
away with his sledge hammer, tiny puffs of plaster dust shot
through the old nail holes in the wall of Assen's apartment.
On a whim, Assen tore up the note terminating his lease. It's
not legal, he said cheerfully through the locked door, and
listened for a while. That's what you think, the landlord said
at last, and went slowly back down the stairs.

Assen received a second note, in which the landlord
offered to find him another apartment. He corrected the
spelling errors and returned it without comment. The local
court authorities indicated that they were overloaded and
wouldn't be able to take up the case before the end of the

following year: so the war between them began. They nodded to each other solemnly on the stairway, like opponents in a duel. Whenever they passed one another, the landlord would spit. He held the door open when Assen left the building so that he could slam it shut behind him, he threw a brick through his bathroom window, dropped burning matches, and once a dead rat, into his mailbox. Assen stuffed the rat into one of the landlord's stray rubber boots, let the air out of the tires of his mo-ped, poured plaster of Paris in his gas tank, and withheld more and more rent each month because of the increasingly annoying dust and noise. When a truckdriver asked him where to dump a load of sand, he sent him to the playground down the block, and watched the landlord trundling a wheelbarrow up and down the street for several days. Sometimes at night, he would look up from his books and see his landlord crouching on the dark ironwork of the scaffolding, staring angrily into his room, motionless. His hands tightened into fists, his chin raised, Assen stared back until the muscles of his face ached from a suppressed grin. Then he would turn the desk lamp on him quickly, at which, spotlighted before all the neighbors, his landlord would slip away silently as a weasel.

*

The telephone rang several times over the next few days, but he didn't answer it. He forced himself to stay home, reading books at random, racing to get through them, longing to read something that would cure him of the constant torment of feeling that he wasn't reading enough, or more precisely, that there wasn't enough time left to read less without worrying about it. In every book he hoped to find some final and definitive explanation, admittedly without having the least notion of what it was he wanted to have explained. The fact that everything he read raised new questions shaping his subsequent reading finally gave him something he could hold on to, albeit shakily; asking questions, he thought, brought him into slightly greater contact with the world. But the answers left him mute. And yet he sought them, and brushed them aside, in order to free his view for his own mystery, or at least its contours, flashing out briefly in the everyday light. Reluctantly he sought a guiding principle for his life, his work, and at times he was frightened by the thought that he had already read, perhaps even written, the decisive sentence, found his personal formula, without realizing it.

As the moon waxed—he saw it shining through a break in the clouds—so too did his restlessness. Heels clicking on the pavement, laughing women from below, plastic bags filled with clinking bottles. Taverns floated within him, and he slipped into his street shoes because his feet were cold. The more he longed to go out, the more senseless his delaying tactics became. He turned the face of his alarm clock to the wall and took the dust jackets off his books so they were easier to hold. He ironed his only tie, sharpened all his pencils, numbered manuscript pages, and was in the act of polishing the doorknob when Iris tapped at his window.

She had climbed up the scaffolding in her tight black dress, costume jewelry, and white leather jacket (her shoes were stuck in her side pockets), and now she was wiping the dust off her hands. She smiled as he opened the window, and held out her cigarette for a light. He tried to climb out, but couldn't find his footing on the window sill until she helped him. She turned her cheek to his kiss: fresh lipstick. Leaning against the steel pipes, they watched the moon, no longer veiled, which Iris called merciless. Merciless? he asked. She didn't reply, she smoked; he saw her face, moonstruck of course, in semiprofile. Fine rays of light, finer than hair, streamed from her rhinestone earrings into the pale dusk, as if her body warmth were flowing through the tiny prisms of the stones out into the falling night.

*

There wasn't a chair free in Lauter's bar, The Right Place, the air conditioner was simply recirculating the smoke, the restroom doors never stopped swinging (one door labeled *Men* in brass letters, the other blank). A champagne bucket filled with white tulips adorned the tap-barrel; in a darker room next door, the restaurant area, candlelight glowed through the beer glasses. Lauter, who was sitting on a bar stool, rolled up a copy of the *Stern* and nodded to Iris in mock politeness. As if he had dismissed her with this gesture, he turned his full attention to Assen.

High-percentage moonshine, he said. Since I've been in the beer business, I have to figure nature in again. The cash flow shows I'm right. It's like God runs his moistened finger over the glass rim of the soul once a month—the song of the soused sirens. It drives the rabble to the bar, moonstruck welfare recipients, white rats. They all want to slop around a bit in other people's lives, and afterward they find out it wasn't life after all. —By the way, did you know that looney comes from luna? No? Then you know nothing about women, my friend. The moment that big yellow eye gleams through the clouds they're nothing but beautiful, and that's it, you can't ask for anything more. They start using their looks like bikers use their elbows. Could you paint yourself up like that with lipstick and eye-liner? Could you dress the way they do? I'm going to start hiring only guys before long. The chicks won't leave you alone until you've had a whiff of them. And the whiff is more and more disappointing. Give them a little rod and piston action and they stop cleaning the ashtrays properly. I'm not hard-hearted enough to throw them out, but I'm not enough of a saint to stand the sight of them the next day either. It's reached the point where I avoid my own bar when certain girls are on duty. You really know how to screw, one of them said to me the other day, and blew smoke in my face. I fired her right there in bed. I don't have to put up with that. Now I've got to be careful not to step in front of her Volkswagen. They're so cold and domineering you can't love them, and that makes them even more cold and domineering, until they finally flip out, and they then do a decent job.

Is this your friend? Iris said.

A table was free now, the waitress brought glasses and a bottle of wine. As she turned away, Lauter slapped her on the bottom; the imprint of his damp hand evaporated slowly from her dark blue leather skirt. —Whenever there's a full moon, he continued, the women's toilet stops up. The bitches throw their rags in, and I'm the one who gets stuck with the mess. Sometimes I seriously wonder why I'm in this shitty business. But whenever I feel strong enough for a different life, I get euphoric and think: Isn't the way I feel the other life I'm looking for? So I stay stuck in the same old rut.

*

Assen had long since given up responding to Lauter's tirades. It wasn't that he had anything to say: Lauter just wanted to talk, particularly when he was drunk, with as few interruptions as possible, and for both sides if at all possible. He bloomed when he talked, if only wanly. He grasped life through the delicate root system of words, when he fell silent his face suddenly grew tired. Yet language seemed to mean little more to him than hot air, whistling through his teeth. That words had power and weight, that they could have serious consequences, struck him as perverse. Everything could just as well sound some other way. If he were taken at his word, if someone reminded him of something he once said, he thought it petty and presumptuous.

He had published a handful of decent stories a few years ago that hardly anyone noticed. Tired of always being short of money, he opened a bar, and when he was no longer in financial need, and the resistances which had motivated him had disappeared, so too did the necessity to write; then his texts turned theoretical. Increasingly colder constructions arose at increasingly greater intervals, brilliantly clever, and it never occurred to him to question the fact that everything he wrote could be dissected, justified, interpreted, explained. —But why, Assen once asked him, did you bother to write it?

*

When Lauter asked Iris's opinion about an affair that was currently in all the papers, he did so merely in order to answer himself. Although he paid little attention to the tabloids or TV programs, Assen knew about it. Guilty or not guilty was the question of the day about a young woman who, during the trial, shot a man who'd raped and murdered her seven-year-old child, a man who was an habitual sex offender and who had already been in prison several times. —I can understand that, Lauter said, even though I'm not a very understanding fellow. Why should a woman obey a law that seems incapable of protecting her child from idiots like that. Having sacrificed her happiness, she refuses to give up her revenge as well, she won't let her rage be tempered by a lukewarm judicial system, she wants to see her child's killer under the earth and not in therapy or in an air-conditioned cell—all that seems to me as human as the murder was beastly. You have the right to show your teeth in our social zoo. But too bad for you if apes' fangs appear among your artificial crowns; then every nose is stuck in a law book. Even if she'd blown up the whole courtroom, I think I'd let her off. Maternal instinct is doubtless as gentle or insistent or logical as moonshine, a dimension beyond the paragraphs of the law.

Nonsense, Iris said, and proceeded to show she knew the case far better than Lauter, which Assen found embarrassing. In general the fact that Lauter was ignoring Iris (a clear sign of his interest) had kindled a vague panic which was now flaring up inside him, and made listening to them a strain. He felt compelled to watch Lauter's face, watch the tiny twitches at the corners of his mouth, the eyes that narrowed to the slits of a knight's helmet, or rolled upward to the ceiling as he cracked his knuckles, as if he was going to give Iris just three more seconds. He wouldn't forgive her easily for speaking up. Where did you dig up this fruit-cake—Assen was braced for the question, but it wasn't asked, perhaps for that very reason. But Lauter acted attentive, nodding with a thoughtful melancholy that seemed to Assen like clear mockery.

The woman's actions, said Iris, had little to do with maternal instincts, in fact they were the very opposite, they were simply barbaric. After all, she'd had two children before the one that was murdered, and put both of them in a state home without a second thought, and even the dead child received more than caresses at her hand when it was alive. Moreover the lack of understanding she showed for the murderer's mental illness revealed a brutality which was hardly one of the characteristics of a good mother. And the fact that the woman was trading on the corpse of her dead child, that she was marketing her supposed despair so cold-bloodedly, selling exclusive rights to her pain to television stations and magazines, practically made her an accessory after the fact. Her vanity was obvious: shooting the man when all public attention was centered on him to put herself in the spotlight, now that she was no longer the center of her child's life. The wide-spread tacit approval given to her for firing the pistol was actually as shocking as the original crime. The more contradictory the social processes involved, the more complicated and confusing they were, the happier the public was to see a quick trial.

Lauter, his head bowed, clapped his hands silently, magisterially. Assen took off his glasses, everything blurred around him, colors dissolved into rays. The two were talking beyond the range of his short-sightedness, and with the disappearance of their detailed image, Lauter's gnawed fingernails, the small clumps of eye shadow in Iris's lashes, their voices faded as well into the general background noise of the bar. He was annoyed that they talked so self-confidently about events they hadn't experienced themselves, events which might have happened quite differently. Their readiness to accept the media's authority upset him like a fist-fight. The umbilical cord to bodily experience had been severed, and the way they took the phantasms of events at face value made them seem like phantoms themselves; the real crime seemed to him no longer the murder they were discussing, but their exchange of opinions about it. To speak of something other than himself, his own pain, his own pretenses, seemed to Assen irksome and presumptuous, an offense resulting in greater and greater pain, and further pretenses. Where, if not under the lid of his own skull, he thought, did the events of each day twist and turn. What else should one lay down one's life for if not for personal myths, those unconscious thoughts which rise within us laying claim to truth. He wanted to see his own body twitching beneath language as beneath an engraver's burin. But Iris and Lauter were probably thankful not to have to talk about themselves, at least they had a topic of conversation. Or were they talking about themselves in an open secret code, in which nothing need be revealed? The murder in Cologne, the earthquake in Umbria, the Chancellor's short trousers, armament, disarmament—were these in the final analysis metaphors of their own personal condition, for which they no longer felt responsible, happy to leave its formulation to others? —Assen could not discover reality in the headlines, at most only circumstantial evidence for it. Things were in fact no doubt quite different. Surrounded by tabloids, he saw a bloodstained worker's cap flitting through the rotary presses. Lauter laughed (a laugh with dirt in the corners). —Hey, Iris said, why are you so disgustingly cynical? I'm too soft-hearted, he heard him answer, I can't afford to be soft in the head too. Soft-headedness would be the death of me.

Assen lived in Schöneberg, near Winterfeldtplatz, where the smell of tear gas was often in the air in those days. The sidewalks were piled with paving stones that cast long shadows beneath the street lamps, with hub-caps and crate boards, and most of the shop windows were boarded up. Some bar owners kept the roller doors lowered halfway, so that you had to stoop over in order to get into the tavern. The barricades were illuminated at night, like Christmas, walls and walls of posters. "When you've finally finished," read one, the slogan of a large brewery. Crowds racing along, street processions bathed in blue light, aquariums full of panicky life, piles of rubbish, smoke—there was some reason for it all but he wasn't particularly interested in what it was.

One day an old acquaintance rang at his apartment door. He had around twenty demonstrators with him, breathless and partially masked, who looked curiously at his den of books as if it were the home of the muses. (An arbor on the battlefield, said one.) Assen offered what he had in his refrigerator: milk, mineral water, a few bottles of wine. They smoked, paced back and forth from room to room in heated conversation, and kept looking out the windows. Two women showered, a city map was spread out and marked with crosses, someone telephoned for bandages and a car, another typed the draft of a handbill on his typewriter. Assen somewhat self-consciously refilled glasses, poured peanuts into small bowls, emptied ashtrays, and listened in on conversations. The German they spoke while waxing indignant over the crimes of the state, a mixture of chewing gum slang and street clichés, seemed to him as bad as most state crimes. (When you're in a fight you don't have time to be a stylist, his acquaintance said.) Two young demonstrators lay on his bed and waited quietly in each other's arms until a squad car passed by outside.

He wasn't particularly moved by what was at stake in this war—his silent bond with the protestors didn't deceive him on that score. *How* the war was conducted, however, sometimes stirred him to an almost murderous rage. From the surrounding balconies, workers in shirt sleeves, children, and screaming women threw flower pots, coal briquettes, and empty whiskey bottles down onto the demonstrators. German shepherds bared their teeth behind apartment windows. A squad of police, swinging their clubs, ran into the crowd at a point where several women were standing with baby buggies. The officers flailed away as if they were attacking not only the demonstrators, but their own scruples as well. The force of a blow lifted one man six inches into the air. Those falling dragged fleeing people with them to the ground, children rolled about like toys on the asphalt, mothers' screams drowned out those of their children. Within a few minutes the intersection was cleared.

He couldn't hold it against the police. That would have been granting them more respect than they deserved. He packed up a few books and took off, traveling into the surrounding countryside, into a fen or swamp, into suburban areas with meadows and village inns.

Once, on the way to the subway station, a man in a uniform called out to him: You can't go that way. I'm just going to the station, Assen yelled back, still walking. Then he found himself surrounded by four officers in battle gear, he could see his puzzled face mirrored in their visors. Pressing forward, they boxed him in with their shields and poked him in the stomach with a hard rubber billy club, gently at first, then with increasing pressure. They probably wanted him to defend himself so they could render him defenseless once and for all. —It can't be, he cried out in a voice that was new to him: Please! —How clear do I have to make it, said the squad leader. The station is closed, you'll have to take the bus. And Assen took the bus.

*

Does it take certain people to turn a life into a story? Lovers? Things weren't going badly enough for him to write anything good, he worked only haphazardly in those days. A steam iron and underwear—he cleared them from the desk to put his feet up and called Iris. He was surprised at how quickly he'd memorized her number. But that didn't mean anything. The woman's beauty strengthened him, it was true, and he swelled with pride when men paused with their beer to their lips when she appeared in the doorway. Distant acquaintances drew near, women he'd longed for in vain suddenly smiled at him. But when she mentioned the word "relationship" he immediately felt depressed. He didn't think about her feelings, and when he thought of her, he experienced nothing but a mild desire. He intentionally ignored her long looks, the earnestness of her embraces. They met once or twice a week for a meal, wine, and bed, a pleasant habit not far removed from a loveless ritual, and yet it was better than nothing. The fact that it wasn't enough for her he considered a basic weakness of her sex.

They talked on the phone practically every day, desultory conversation with little to say, verbal costume jewelry, superficial chatter. When they weren't face to face they talked randomly, which made sense to him compared to the verbal ping-pong that allowed them to maneuver their way from the bar into a state of agreement with bed in the offing. Iris spoke of this and that—a raw schnitzel that fell out a kitchen window onto the street, six egg cups for one mark sixty, taking a taxi to the demonstration. He recalled her tales of missing curtain rings, a torn hair ribbon, a borrowed sewing machine, stories she seemed to take quite seriously precisely because of their everyday quality, and which she related as if they represented some deep mystery.

He would have liked to tell stories that randomly, without worrying about whether the other person was paying attention. Speech was evidently organic in her case. Assen, for the most part, simply performed operations with it. With each experience, each event, came immediate doubt about its validity. As a rule he considered them too minor to be worth relating, was too little involved with them to bother with their expression. He was so shamed by Iris's automatic assumption that he was listening that in spite of his lazy tendency toward distraction, he actually paid attention.

When they fell silent—and they were silent for long periods, saying enough to one another in their silence—he heard other callers arguing indistinctly in the background. Or there would be a crackling, as if a weather front were moving in between their phones; Iris was striking a match. Huskily, pretending to be hoarse, but his voice soon husky enough, he talked to her about her body. Taking long, deep, and audible breaths, she seemed to inhale what he was saying, a verbal cosmetic. Where would we be without the telephone, he asked, and heard the sound her stockings made when she crossed her legs. Apart, she said.

She surprised him with gifts that he accepted at first because he didn't want to offend her. But he soon began offending her in order to stop them. She gave him whatever it was she'd bought with the same smug smile, almost solemnly, each one a trump she was playing, lifting her chin in anticipation as he tore open the package. A fountain pen, a walkman, ties. He reacted far too happily, and felt the false joy as a tension in his face, as if he were smiling with the same muscles he used to bare his teeth. She bought him underwear, shaving items, household utensils, and when he asked her not to, she simply waved him aside, as if she didn't want to hear about it, as if she knew what was really good for him. She reproached him wordlessly for his unkindness with a new watch, art books, or expensive wine. And she underlined the fact that he never brought her flowers by always bringing fresh ones for him.

He tossed a bouquet of anemones into the toilet before her eyes; he found a small blue package tied with a gold ribbon hanging on his door and threw it away unopened.

*

But when he rang at her door one day without any advance warning, her face said that everything was all right again. He stepped quickly into the entrance and refused to remove his coat. She grabbed him by the shoulders, kissed him, and rolled her eyes upward in laughing inquiry, as if she could read the brand of his liquor on the ceiling. He hadn't been drinking. He walked around her apartment straightening vases and rugs, closed a cabinet door, and tapped a crooked picture so sharply that he knocked it from the wall. —Would you like some tea, oh yes, you take coffee, don't sit on that sewing stuff, now where was I? She lit a candle, gave him a glass of wine, and brought out her picture albums, uncles, sisters, her dead father. He leaned back on the couch and let her show them to him. The more meaningfully he eyed her, the more rapidly she spoke, and the more stories occurred to her about the pictures, the simplest of which now seemed important. Her cheeks glowed, she was like an eager child who doesn't want to go to bed. When he thought he'd almost reached his goal, he saw her yet another cigarette length away. Finally he ran his thumb down her spine; she straightened up and then it was an easy matter to topple her.

So all you wanted to do was sleep with me, she said, as he was getting dressed afterward. What about you, he asked, did you sleep with me without really wanting to, like a whore?

*

They were sitting on a bench in the subway station, Iris seemed to be in a bad mood. At any rate she wouldn't look at him, stared into the tunnel, and didn't respond when he offered her a cigarette. Intimidated by her ill humor, he asked her if anything was wrong so softly that the loudness of her answer seemed in itself a reprimand. —What do you *think* is wrong, she replied in a tone that showed his total lack of understanding: I'm bleeding. He turned his face away in shock. He hadn't wanted to know the intimate details. It was as if she had told him her family name for the first time.

He recalled a morning from his childhood when his mother had overslept and he had to wake her to fix his school lunch. She threw the covers back as if her boss had called; he stared in fascination at the large stains of dried blood on the sheets and her nightgown. She sent him from the room without explaining anything, and because she didn't seem sick or wounded, he thought what he'd seen was excrement. The thought that his shiny clean mother had dirtied her bed made her seem less threatening for a few moments. Or had she been shot in a dream? But he never dared to ask her about the spots, for he sensed that she was embarrassed, and he was afraid to remind her of her shame for fear she would fly into a rage.

Iris jumped up, hung her purse over his shoulder, and ran past the glass window of the subway office, where two drunks were singing. With a cry, she hugged a young pregnant woman who had just carried a baby buggy down the stairs. After exchanging a few words Assen couldn't hear, the friend put her hands on her hips and stuck out her stomach toward Iris, apparently in answer to a question. Iris laughed, blushing as she did so, and they both stuck their heads under the sunshade of the baby buggy.

Open up, yelled one of the drunks, who was dressed in lederhosen and a sleeveless jean jacket, open the fodder shoot. He banged on the glass partition with the flat of his hand, the subway official behind grinned uncomfortably and crossed his arms.

Back when he was a child, Assen always felt they were hiding something from him when the girls were excused from gym or swimming. What was their problem, since nothing seemed to be wrong with them? In later years he thought monthly periods were one reason girls got along so well together, something he always envied about them. They would leave the classroom hand in hand, while his neighbor would be hitting him in the back. Wounded for some dark reason, they seemed already mature by the age of twelve or thirteen, they had a knowing look that made the teachers nervous or strict. And yet for a long time he didn't understand that there was a connection between the beautiful women he saw outlined in the spring sun and the bloody tampon he once found floating in the gutter, swollen thick as a rat by the rain.

When, at fourteen, he fell in love for the first time, his

mother showed a new and therefore disturbing tendency to take him into her confidence. This woman, whom he had never seen in anything but long dresses and blouses buttoned to the neck (he couldn't imagine her naked beneath her clothes), who tersely ordered everyone in the family to lock the bathroom door when they were in there, who took every speck of dirt personally, and even perfumed the water in the toilet bowl, now told him about her most intimate indispositions, often at breakfast, with her house robe askew, about her digestive problems and the consistency of her feces, about her "greasy periods"—a term she seemed to use with a special, bitter pleasure—about her various discharges, the spots on her underwear and on the bed, about the smell and degree of clarity of her urine. If he showed his disgust she went on in even greater and more breathless detail, her small, hard eyes opened wide. Although he always listened politely, suppressing his nausea, her revelations still struck him like a blow to the stomach, as an attempt to drive his girlfriend from him by any means, to disgust him with everything about women, and to end the fascination she sensed in him.

*

One of the drunks—with shoulder-length, straw-yellow hair and a tobacco-stained mustache above a gaping mouth with missing teeth—had drawn near without his having noticed, and now sat down on Assen's lap. Listen, man . . . a tattooed tear dripped from each cloudy eye with its milky glaze, a six-inch wound, recently stitched, ran across his forehead, the thread ends still protruding. Assen tried to dump the man off his lap, but he was gripping the back of the bench with both hands. —Don't do that, man. He seemed amused. —Give me a mark and I'll go away. Assen cast a sidelong glance at the people standing around, no one seemed to notice anything; they picked lint from their coats, glanced at their watches. He was too surprised to feel afraid, but the thought of Iris seeing him in this humiliating position made him blush furiously. —All right, all right, but first get off my lap. The man stood up and put his arm around his buddy who had walked up. —This sweetie-pie—he tapped the pink strap of Iris's purse—is going to give us a little bread. How nice, the other one said, and held out his hand to Assen. Looking up at both of them as from a well, he heard the rumble of the train approaching through the tunnel.

He knew too little about these men as human beings, and knew them perhaps too well as types, to feel contempt or even hate for them. But he wasn't just ashamed of being their victim, his red face was as embarrassing to him as an open fly, and it made him so angry he decided not to give them a cent. —What can I do for you, he asked, as if there were a desk between them, and crossed his arms on his chest. —What, said the man with the scar, thrown for a moment by this small break in the script. Didn't you promise . . . But he was already grinning again, and slapped Assen lightly on the mouth with the back of his hand, on which a rose was tattooed. Assen took a deep breath and stood up. Watch it, he said with a voice that fluttered away from him as he spoke. He gave the man a shove that sent him back a step. Watch it, the other said mockingly in a prim voice, and shoved Assen back into the other man, who caught him against his broad chest. He laughed and cried out in fake indignation: Watch it! He knocked Assen back with both fists just as two trains shot out of the tunnel with partially opened doors through which the passengers were already peering. To catch himself, but also to avoid being hit again, Assen stumbled with raised fists toward the scarred man, who stepped back quickly and tripped him, sending him tumbling into one of the passengers who suddenly filled the long platform. A formless wave of people directed by loudspeakers toward the exits inundated all cross traffic, and he let himself be pushed along gratefully beyond the reach of both bikers. There was a loud crash as glass broke somewhere, and a woman cried out shrilly: Watch it there!

He met Iris again in the middle of the platform and they got into the train. After waving good-bye to her friend, who was leaving on the other train, she pointed to the corner of his mouth in shock. What do you *think* is wrong, he said, looking at his red fingertips, I'm bleeding.

*

A beautiful woman, Lauter said, or what we generally think of as one, is like a fascinating poster. You look at it and you're delighted. And no matter how you twist and turn her, a beautiful woman is still beautiful, even when she's in despair, even with a runny nose and tear-filled eyes she still looks like a dream. That gets old quickly, doesn't it? But a plain woman, one whose beauty has to be discovered in her gestures and movements (because they're all *beautiful* of course, an angel hovers in every soul)—a woman like that is as inexhaustible as an oil painting. While the foregrounded one tires our eyes with her splendor, only to become increasingly flat and insipid, a poster after all, good at most for surprises and swindles, the plain one brings greater pleasure each time you see her. You see something new to attract you every time: the line of her neck in the early morning light, the curve of her loins in a particular position, a vacant smile, astonishingly clever eyes; the golden child shimmers constantly through the coat of the gray mouse. And since she isn't constantly sought after, sex hasn't become boring and disgusting, she still has a healthy longing and pulls you to bed happily by the tail. She simply gives you more than the flash-bulb faces: you're not just the person enjoying her beauty, you've *discovered* her. And that's a breath of seventh heaven. On the other hand: they're all monsters of course, the cross we nail ourselves to every night. I had one once that must have had teeth in her moss.

*

The sun shone through a honey jar next to half a roll, a Brandenburg Concerto on the radio. Iris, silhouetted against the light, smoking. Assen couldn't recognize her face, only the clip-on earring of gilded tin, the size of a coin. —Well what about it, she asked, do you want to work or shall we do something. She stubbed out her cigarette in the egg cup and crossed her legs. What annoyed him about a question like that was that it sounded like: Do you want to fantasize, or shall we do something normal. He'd already accustomed himself to her grin, her silent disdain for his work, it was fine with him in fact, since it spared him having to talk about something he neither cared to explain nor could. (The energy he expended talking about writing would only be lost to him later when he wrote). The depressing thing about Iris's question was that it was one of the innumerable threads she wove into a web of "relationships," a warm nest, a cozy home, which he could only tear apart. And of course it was his fault when she ran into his knife, why did he have a knife? A few days ago she'd looked at him quietly, quietly through her tears, and shattered a cognac glass in her bare hand.

Things had now reached the point where she allowed him to "work." She would get up with an oh, yeah, or see you later then, and he would stay behind, penitent and contrite, the way she wanted him. The fact that he had his scruples about disappointing or wounding her made her unscrupulous in her choice of weapons. Her wishes soon seemed to him nothing more than a layer of varnish over her curses, which would break through if he indulged his idiosyncrasies, splintering the surface, although fairly quietly: a twitch at the corner of her mouth, a split-second narrowing of her eyes, a brief snort. He poured some champagne in the empty coffee cups. She wanted to make a Sunday man of him, he could sense it. How about miniature golf? MINIATURE GOLF? he roared into her startled face. And the desire to yield he already felt, the attraction, that syrupy feeling in his chest? Oh well, he said with a warmth that actually carried him away. Let's do something normal and fantasize a bit.

He knelt before her amused gaze and unfastened her garters with his teeth.

*

Once when she noted her surprise that he had no friends except Lauter, he had the uncanny feeling for an instant that she was shoving her foot in his door. A person needed friends: she confronted him with it like an easily learned psychotherapeutic rule, which immediately made him hostile. Having friends was evidently proof to her of something, perhaps of sociability (not a word to him, but a signal to start retching).

Of course he knew that he took himself too seriously, that he weighed himself down with his own concerns, that in the end he would have to look away from his own person if he really wanted to see himself. (He was narcissistic even in self-laceration, accused himself only to acquit himself, turned up the dirt of his character, relentlessly thorough, only to sweep it immediately back under the rug. He would decide that he was a bad person, basically impossible, simply so that he could console himself in the next instant that he wasn't really all that bad.) The older he got the easier he found it to do without friends. Sooner or later he always held it against them that they weren't what he wanted himself to be—a feeling that bothered him more than them. He hardly met anyone anymore who could open up fully and without reservation, and was strong enough *not* to build up their power at the expense of the other's weakness. And if he had to remain alone with his secret thoughts even in a friendship, then what was the point of friendship. He just didn't want to be left speechless again by the same old thing: the moment you left yourself open, you could guarantee that there would be someone right there ready to stick a well-meaning knife into you.

Iris's remark was a knife too, one of the countless cuts she inflicted on him to whittle him down until only a portion remained, one she could stick comfortably into her pocket.

As a punishment, he didn't spend the night with her, which caused him to fall upon her even more passionately at the next opportunity, and for the first time he felt taken to her breast in earnest.

*

More and more often he would flee the blankness of a sheet of paper to spend time with her. And the more out of place he felt at her side, the more he was driven to prove himself to her. In order to impress her, he would gild even his smallest professional successes. He had the bad taste to give her a magazine containing a text by him (she never mentioned it again), and took her to an exhibition by an artist whose work he'd once analyzed in an essay. In front of each picture she would cast an expectant sidelong glance at Assen, the expert who didn't have a clue about anything in real life. She moved on to the next picture while he was still talking, and continued on that way until he finally lost sight of her. She was waiting for him at the cloakroom with his coat over her arm.

He forced himself not to call her until she called him, but he answered on the first ring. They went to the movies, arrived a little late, and had to sit apart. He'd embraced her while they were outside at the box office, she was soft and yielding in her white wool dress, her look seductive and menacing at the same time. Now, in the darkness, he saw the back of her head a few rows in front of him, a fuzzy glow surrounding her hair. She wouldn't be thinking of him now; he was already beginning to resent the film because of it. "I'm going to see a man about a dog," he grinned at the phrase, and imagined what it would be like to disappear without a trace from the theater, from the city, into another life, where he would be free from the magic of her skin, from the humiliation of his desire.

He waited for a while outside before Iris appeared in the entrance. She was talking with someone putting on a motorcycle helmet, and gave him a page from her notebook. Before getting on his machine, he waved to her, ponderously, like a cosmonaut, and she beamed.

Assen suggested they go somewhere and have a drink. She didn't answer right away, stared after the rear light of the motorcycle, and her final "All right then" sounded as if she were giving him one more chance.

Without another word she pushed him into a discotheque. His objection was immediately swallowed by music as she opened the door, an electronic noise that made him think of reinforced nerve fibers being plucked in a dead body. They sat at the bar in their coats. You couldn't talk to anyone here, it was dance or drink, there was little or nothing in between, and although Iris squeezed his hand a few times, he felt rejected. He saw people swirled around by sound as in a centrifuge, expelling everything but the material bodies themselves. At one point one of the speakers went dead and for a few seconds his left ear seemed deaf, as if a switch had been thrown in his head and only half his brain still functioned.

After the second glass of wine they shed their coats and Iris shoved him onto the dance floor. Nothing seemed more absurd at that moment. He would have liked to have pulled her out of the bar again and shaken her until the words he longed for fizzed out of her. He could tell she realized that by the fact that you wouldn't think she knew by looking at her. His hands on his hips, he stood before her, leaning over slightly in his oversized suit. She looked him gravely in the eyes and, almost imperceptibly, began to dance. Standing in place, she swayed her legs and hips. He imagined her body humming. She bit her lower lip and moved her shoulders left and right, still cautiously. Assen felt paralyzed by embarrassment, a spotlight cast their long shadows across the empty dance floor. He glanced sideways at the others around them, but could see only their silhouettes in this light, the glow of their cigarettes, no one dancing; the notes were only a lead-in. Iris raised her hands, snapped her fingers. She seemed to know the slow and threatening crescendo of the piece well, for at the precise moment a saxophone pierced through the beat, she pulled at Assen's arm. He stood rigidly, the top half of his body sharply turned, his tie swinging loosely. He took a breath, a gasp of air. As the drummer hit the cymbals, Iris spun him about full force with the flat of her hand. Whirling around, he braced his feet solidly on the metal dance floor. He felt out of joint with his own muscular system. She smiled and danced on unperturbed. Her movements now scarcely harmonized with the searching rhythms, the sounds arriving from far away. They were the nervous flickering premonition of a melody that no one could hear but her. A glass shattered in stereo, a trombone emerged from nowhere and flared above their heads. The piece broke off for a few beats.

Iris closed her eyes, tilting her head to one side. Her face was pale, abandoned to the silence, he wanted to kiss her. Then she parted her lips, her teeth were clenched, she wrinkled her nose, grabbed his tie, and, just as the music rolled up behind them like a huge, silent wave and broke across the dance floor, glass green and translucent, she slapped his face smartly.

Then she danced away. His ears were ringing, he had trouble keeping his balance, and he stumbled toward her, loosening his tie. He tried to make his way through the thicket of dancing bodies that now filled the entire dance floor, but he kept being pushed aside. A bald woman with a man's coiffure painted on her head drove him away by stabbing at him with a burning cigarette. He craned his neck, saw Iris at the opposite end of the room, a strand of blond hair in her face, glowing points of light in her eyes, a pair of self-reflecting spotlights. She looked sad even though she was dancing, and he thought of leaving. The loudspeakers fell silent again, the disk jockey ran his fingers through his hair. A grainy murmur arose, and suddenly Assen had the feeling—it was more distinct than any phrase could ever be, and basically more subtle than feeling, a sensation that flashed for a second through a mysterious gap—that the universe had paused for a single heartbeat to allow the momentary and yet eternally true reconciliation of all conflicts through his affection for Iris.

If he wanted to reach her he would have to dance his way there, that was clear. He merged into the crowd, which, in spite of the silence, was still pulsating with clattering heels and jangling jewelry, and floated almost effortlessly toward her. She caressed the spot she had just slapped, hugged him, and kissed him lightly—and as the music stuttered forth again, they began a long dance which stretched out to include even the pauses while the records were being changed; in his breathlessness it seemed to him they wanted to use the dance to escape their bodies through a previously unknown inner ardor, to dissolve in the melodies, in each drop of sweat sparkling on their faces; a dance in which Assen saw nothing but Iris's eyes, her occasional smile, and his tie, which twirled like the hand of a clock gone wild.

*

That night hail threshed all the blossoms from the chestnut trees. They looked plucked and disconsolate in the early morning light and yet they were now filled with tiny nuts. Assen drove a taxi for a few days to earn some extra money; tired of the cold spells which had lasted into late spring, he thought of taking a trip, perhaps to the seaside.

Many of his fares sank into the cushioned seats with a happy sigh, still immersed in their own thoughts or something they'd done, still recalling conversations with flushed faces and blank stares before they called out their destinations. In their case too, summer announced itself in an apparent decision not to put up with spring anymore. Their clothes were distinctly bright, distinctly comfortable, and too light-weight, several of them had head colds and sniffed their noses defiantly. Sitting in the middle of the back seat, stretching their arms out on the top of the seat and humming as they gazed into the bustling traffic, they gave the impression of already being on vacation from their every-day lives. Riding itself seemed to remove exactly that weight from experience which was normally painful.

He telephoned Iris without reaching her. Straining as if to hear her approaching steps beyond the sound of the phone, he listened to the ringing in the receiver until it grew softer and softer and the beat of his pulse in his ear louder and louder. His thoughts of her were filled with tender rage, a feeling that made his cheekbones hurt. When, one cigarette later, he started to pick up the receiver again, he crossed his arms in annoyance, but forgot himself an instant later and was rubbing his shoulders. His hands awakened the memory of her skin, a few words flashed through his mind in her voice.

One night when he'd stopped in front of her building in his taxi and was staring at the darkened windows of her apartment, he heard the telephone ring behind the curtains and imagined to himself that *he* was the one calling, from the time before he knew her, or knew only his longing for her, and had "mis-dialed."

The next morning he was awakened by an express mail messenger. Iris was at her sister's house near Florence and enclosed a check for the train ticket and a description of how to get there. The highway which twisted through hills and forests in ball point pen led to a lipstick kiss.

*

There were long lines at the ticket counters. Two Turks in orange overalls were sweeping out the station—the older one, who had a thick mustache and a padded crease above the bridge of his nose, with quick and practiced motions, swath by swath; the younger one smooth-shaven with a stylish hairdo, relaxed, careless, smoking. He stopped repeatedly to eye various women. The older one warned him several times—not loudly, but sounding nervous and worried, as if a supervisor were standing somewhere nearby. That didn't seem to impress the young man; he leaned his broom against a column, pulled a small radio from his pocket, and began untangling the cord for the earphone. Now the old man threw his broom down, the handle struck the floor with a surprisingly loud bang, the people waiting in line turned their heads. He strode over with raised fists to his colleague, who slipped away from him with a grin and put the radio back to his ear immediately. Then the older man grabbed him with both hands, swung him around, and pulled the front of his overalls tight at the chest.

Where do you think you are, he yelled, looking quickly at those in line. In a nightclub? Do you want your money for free, you miserable Turk, and child welfare too? The young man lowered his head in embarrassment and said something to him in their own language that the old man evidently didn't want to hear; he grabbed him even more tightly by the front. You're supposed to be sweeping, can't you understand German? Well? He looked at those in line with theatrical indignation. He doesn't understand a word of German, he said, it's getting worse and worse. —What do you want here? Big cars? Blond women? Disco? The youngster looked down at the floor and grinned. Disco, that's a word he understands, the old man cried, give me some music. Disco, his homeland! But here, he struck himself on the chest—in his heart it stinks of the sheep stall. He's so dumb the ducks would trample him dead, he can't even sweep, a typical Kurd. You can't give 'em a knife in a restaurant for fear they'll cut themselves. You hear? Do you want people to think all Turks are lazy? Then head for the pampas, my friend! We're humans just like everyone else, we have toothaches and coffee, we pay our taxes. Get with it or get out. We don't want everybody talking about dirty foreigners; keep people friendly, A-One, you Kanaka. Are you ready to sweep now? He placed his hands on his hips and repeated the question in Turkish; the young man, who was apparently beginning to grow fearful of his colleague, nodded hesitantly; he looked him in the eye as he did so. — All right then—the old man turned to those waiting in line and turned his palms up: Now he's ready to sweep.

The bus that Assen found waiting in front of the railway station in Florence took him as far as Seano, a small town near Bacchereto, the closest village to her house. The remnants of sunset glowed at the end of the country road. Blue-black clouds, beneath which white-throated swallows sailed, moved slowly across the sky, and everything seemed outlined with doubled sharpness against the darkness. Assen could see individual tufts of grass growing from windowsills and in the gutters; a pale yellow house, not much bigger than a garage, gleamed majestically. A woman called out a name, a long, drawn-out call across the hills; a child came walking by and proudly showed him a large marble: milk-white glass with honey-colored spirals. Gusts of wind whipped through the vines of the surrounding fields, turn-ing up the light green undersides of the leaves, which shimmered a metallic blue beneath the threatening sky. In an inner courtyard, which Assen saw through a dark cow barn filled with the uneasy sound of clinking chains, a young woman in a poppy-red apron was washing out wooden troughs. Behind a wall of glass bricks a fire burned. A rumble rolled through the space above the clouds and ended abruptly, as if it had been swallowed. A flag that had been snapping loudly a moment before fell limply on its pole; a furze bush standing in the same yard righted itself as the wind dropped suddenly. Bits of paper whirling in the air floated back to the asphalt and lay motionless, on an ivy-covered gable not a leaf stirred. Yet on the horizon the storm whipped a cluster of cypresses beneath a bright gray shimmering light.

The first clap of thunder, still subdued, was followed by a silent flash of lightning above the vineyard and, a split second later, a loud crack painful to the ears. A few large drops of rain fell into the dust, and then at last a soft, even rain began falling heavily, so quietly that it seemed to have nothing to do with the rumbling, rending, and rattling in the clouds. The water was already pouring in streams from the gutters and tinkling into bottles standing about. The windows fogged over. An earth-brown brew slopped over the edges of the flowerpots which lined the balconies, and plants with their roots washed white lay scattered about on the asphalt.

Assen, who owned neither umbrella nor raincoat, did not seek shelter. He strode along singing at the edge of the road, his water-soaked shoes squishing at each step. A flash of lightning illuminated a garden behind a yew hedge, the red caps of stone dwarfs in the grass; a dripping felt hat adorned the head of a life-size ceramic deer. The lights of a truck that came roaring by in a huge cloud of spray flowed dazzlingly across the lenses of his glasses. His trousers clung to his skin, but he only felt the cold at the level of a few coins in his pockets. Through the lit door of a barn stall he saw the bared teeth of a horse, which, with the black nostrils above them, seemed like a death's-head. From the wreckage of an auto in the ditch, which probably saw no survivors, three puppies stared out at him. A white plastic sack was caught in the top of a tall cypress, violet strands of vapor floated over the vineyards. He stopped once to stand for a while beneath one of the many pine trees which grew at the side of the road and allowed hardly a drop of water through. He smoked a cigarette, the pack still dry in his traveling bag. Motionless, as if the weather were far too bad to worry about him, ringdoves stared down from the branches, and a solitary, thickly-ruffled raven opened its beak. But that happened later, in a dream, when Assen passed that way again.

When, an hour later, he reached Bacchereto, it had stopped raining. Gurgling and glittering, the flowing water sought its level, and children playing in the street stared at him as if he had arisen from the river. A few of them held ruby-red suckers through which the street lamps gleamed. In the tavern where Assen had coffee and a drink, they told him the way to the house of the *signorina tedesca*. But he still got lost on the paths across the countryside. He could distinguish nothing beneath the starless, inky heavens but a few scattered white stones and once the rear end of a rabbit hopping away. He heard but could not see the rustling trees. The illuminated window toward which he finally climbed along a slope planted with olive trees—the damp earth clinging heavily to his shoes—belonged to a small dyeworks. In a pale blue haze, in which a few light bulbs were burning, men and women were standing at hip-high vats, stirring them with poles. Several rows of thick winter sweaters were hanging on a wall, blue; an old woman was nimbly stitching gold colored labels onto the collars. A baby was sleeping in a yellow plastic tub. A man dried off his stained lower arms, stepped outside the building with Assen, and with a few rapid words pointed in a direction in which nothing could be seen but the night. As he noticed Assen's bewildered stare, he laughed and waved him into his car, switching on the headlights by banging his fist on the dashboard.

He made his way down the hill in first gear, the headlight beams disappearing into the clouds. The tires kept spinning in the mud, and once the car slipped sideways toward the edge of the hill, at the foot of which Assen saw tiny street lamps. Shifting gears constantly, the man talked on, not in the least disturbed that Assen understood almost nothing of what he said. They drove a short way across the gravel bed of a shallow stream, then, pursued silently by three dogs, across a dark farmyard and then uphill again in a series of steep curves through an olive grove. The silvery foliage glittered in the moonlight, a cat jumped almost straight up as they passed. Ragged and peaceful now, the clouds floated away behind the narrow house which reared up blackly before them, and the man turned into a small courtyard. He asked shyly for a smoke, something German, *originale*. When Assen tried to give him the whole pack, he refused and took two cigarettes. He drove rapidly back down the hill, and Assen, happy to have finally reached his goal, saw in the repeated flare of his brake lights a parting greeting.

The house was a windowless dark as far as he could tell. Nearby stood an open shed in which farm tools gleamed, rakes, sickles. A Solex was leaning against a pine tree, an orange stuck in the opening of the broken headlamp. A flight of large, uncut fieldstone steps led up a grassy slope, and as he stepped onto the unexpected dip of the stairs, worn away over generations, he felt himself merge happily into the house's surroundings. He went around the corner of the wall and found himself reflected in a glass door behind which candles were burning. Inside the room, on a table, he noticed a loaf of bread, onions, and the blackish red of a wine bottle. His first step into the kitchen crushed a red pepper lying on the cool floor with other vegetables. A mouse disappeared without haste under the woodpile by the stove. The tiles were loose, and creaked no matter how carefully he walked. From the upper story, down a stairway stacked with books, Iris rushed to him on wooden clogs.

His eyes narrowed to slits, satisfied, exhausted, he gladly accepted her excited, affectionate welcome. She drew a bath and gave him dry clothes and warm shoes of woven straw. She cooked eggs and rice and smoked while she watched him eat. They smiled repeatedly at each other, and because he was so hungry he wanted to gulp his food down, he deliberately chewed slowly. An awkward feeling, an expectant silence arose between them, and after a few hesitant, almost polite questions and answers, it forced from them a long, babbling stream of speech in which everything seemed significant, reviving them once more. Assen couldn't stop looking at Iris, he found new beauties in her face, which in spite of being totally sympathetic, still intimidated him somewhat. The shadows of her gesticulating hands flickered through the room, the flame of his lighter gleamed in her pupils, and suddenly it was clear to him that this tender voice, this smile, the beautiful traits with which Iris held him in her power, were an exact mirror image of the pains which would one day drive him to despair. Alone.

*

Do you know what time it is? Eternity. Dried flowers were pressed behind the glass of the clock on the wall. The sun stood over the open house, through which birds flew and shadows wandered. The whole valley smelled of fresh-mown grass. Early June was already unusually hot, forest fires were expected in the course of the summer. On nearby Monte Albano a caterpillar tractor cut paths into the woods for the fire-fighters. You could hear the screech for days, the straining engine, the trees snapping.

Assen lay in the grass with the neighbor's chickens, drinking white, ice-cooled wine and smoking more than was good for him. He read: the poetry of Montale, the Upanishads, Highsmith. He was relaxed but alert, and hummed melodies as he read. A type of vetch had grown up the side of a cypress, permeating its profound green with tiny blossoms. (*Pines,* said Iris, the word sounds like cypresses look.) Colors struck him as never before: a blue towel on a red plastic line, the glassy green roof tiles of a white house, the multiple grays and browns of the doves, and for the first time since he was in school, he had the urge to paint. He was amazed. Was there some compelling inspiration in colors, overflowing the limits of form, which moved the spectator to reproduce them beneath these skies? Iris came back from the village, she was wearing a white dress. Its buttons were red like the vetch.

She laid an apple with a bite missing on his book and stuck out her tongue. He watched her go, her special way of walking, which had charmed him as long as he had known her. At each slow step with her toes turned out slightly, her lower body seemed to swing forward, while her shoulders tilted back, her arms relaxed and dangling. Once when he was secretly imitating this walk, he immediately felt a faint but insistent sexual excitement. He straightened up, saw her pass through the bright kitchen, naked, into the bath. Her skin glistened with sweat and momentarily reflected the green of the sun-drenched acacias beyond the door. He didn't understand what she said, he just heard her voice, just as he saw not the valley but its breadth, not the heavens in which the wings of the dragonfly flashed, but its infinite amplitude. Iris stood bending over the tub and looked back at him with a smile.

*

Who wrote that there could be no true life in falsity? In any case he realized that only a person who was living "truly" could write such a sentence. Sometimes the only thing missing from his happiness was someone to thank for it.

*

The cherries were ripe, the village children climbed into the foliage with earphones or hung transistor radios from the branches. Boxes full of fruit stood scattered all about the hillside. Iris was wearing a black slip, with a garnet necklace wrapped around her ankle. She sat on the doorstep painting a chair. —Cherries, she said, staring at the white paint dripping from the brush, bring back bad memories. The orphanage they shipped my sister and me to right from our mother's grave stood in a cloud of blossoming cherry trees. It never really got dark in the dormitory in the spring, so that we always whispered until the shadow of one of the sisters appeared. She banged her cane on the beds and ordered us to get to sleep. By the way, do you know why I eat so fast, why I gulp everything down? There wasn't ever enough dessert for everyone in the home, you only got some if you were among the first to finish the main course, which was always the boys of course. We had to help harvest the cherries each June, and one time I put on a jogging suit that had elastic bands around the ankles. I stuffed them full of cherries for my sister and me, sneaked away, and deposited the loot in our beds. To make sure she didn't give anything away, and because I wanted it to be a surprise, I didn't tell my sister anything. But at vespers I started worrying that she might be too startled, or throw the bed covers back too

far, and give us away. I made signs to her (we were separated
into age groups). I folded my hands and laid my cheek
against them, like this. She nodded. So she understood bed.
But how could I make clear to her about the cherries. I stuck
a few pretend ones in my mouth and chewed around on
them, but she shook her head. She'd received some caramels
for penmanship and probably thought I wanted to share
them with her. Then I made a V with the fingers of both
hands, like this: two cherries hanging together on attached
stems. I placed them behind my ears and nodded at her. She
smiled with all her missing teeth and nodded back with two-
finger V's behind her ears. So the cherries were clear too.
Now of course the others had noticed us—there was whispering, snickering, and the creaking of chairs—and suddenly pairs of children in every row nodding to each other
with finger-V's behind their ears. But the Lord God, by
some miracle, was looking elsewhere. I was still in the
washroom brushing my teeth when I heard my sister
scream. I could imagine what had happened. She'd jumped
into bed without looking, squashed the cherries, and now
she saw her nightgown covered all over with blood, the silly
goose. There were screams everywhere, as if a bomb had
gone off, and sisters hurrying through the aisles in their
gray habits, looking like huge roaches. And do you know
what they did with me after they remade the beds? The
Mother Superior pulled me into her office by the ear and
locked the door. She took the picture of the Madonna down
from the wall, crossed herself, and removed it from the
frame. Then she put the frame on the floor and shook hard
peas into the rectangle (it might have been cherry pits or

beans, I don't remember exactly), until they filled it entirely. Then, while she read a book, utterly at peace, I had to kneel on them for one full hour. At first it didn't seem any worse than the pews at High Mass. But after a few minutes I felt every pea, as if thin steel rods were being driven up through my knees and on slowly through my whole body. The more restlessly I shifted about in pain, the more painful it was, I felt like I was about to explode, the roots of my hair were on fire. The hand of the wall clock seemed to have frozen beneath my imploring glance, my pulse pounded in my head as if it were going to break through my eardrum. I bit my lips to keep from crying. And when I was finally allowed to stand up, I couldn't. I crept on all fours into my bed. They never saw a tear.

*

Isn't what we like about a landscape, about the country-side in general, simply the reflection of an unadmitted despair that it doesn't really exist anymore? —Oh yes, Iris said, and threw a biscuit at a proudly striding cock, sending it into the air like a flame—you're lying on a hill outside of Florence and you sound like you're holed up in a bomb crater. If we were in paradise you'd shoot yourself for happiness.

Her hair still wet from the shower, she lay beside him in the tall grass and loosened the red towel she had wrapped around her. The grass which rose high above her body and the branches of a nearby furze cast a net of light and shadow over her skin, her eyes were a watery blue. She tugged at his belt. A few minutes earlier he'd seen a farmer in the adjoining olive grove. He told her and turned over on his stomach to continue reading. In the farmyard below, within shouting distance, he noticed two women, both gray haired, bent over with the effort of hauling a large aluminum tub full of steaming water into the sun. A child around ten years of age, shaved bald and in a jogging suit, leaned two ladders against a white wall. As he raised his head above the grass to follow what was going on, Iris shoved her knee under him and rubbed her face in the hair of his chest. She grabbed for his belt again, and while he held one of her hands tight, balanced on one elbow, she undid his zipper with the other. In the farmyard, the child kicked over a yellow plastic bowl beside the tub, and gazed with folded arms toward the barn door from which the women dragged a pig just as Iris forced herself under him completely. Each of them had hold of one of the pig's ears, its front legs were tied together, they jerked it along toward the steaming tub. Things didn't seem to be going quickly enough for the child—was it a boy or a girl—who, drawing only a hoarse squeak from its constricted throat, kicked the pig in the left rear leg, which was black, wrapped in black, it seemed, in some sort of bandage. Now it bounded forward, skipped past the tub almost into the meadow, so that the women, their faces red with the effort, had to pull it back with all their strength. Assen felt Iris's fingertips on his body, a fleeting series of caresses weaving a net about him, her lips soft and warm on his neck. His arms, braced against the earth, began to tremble, he closed his eyes. When he opened them again, the child was squatting with a cigarette in the corner of its mouth behind the pig, holding the unwrapped leg, while one of the women gath-

ered up her skirt and stood astride the animal as if she
planned to ride it, clamped its head between her doughy
white, blue-veined legs, and held it by the ears. He couldn't
help but smile: the pig's head, which looked out from
beneath the woman's skirt with open mouth, jerked in
shock, something flashed in its face, at the very moment
when Iris pulled him into herself with a little cry. She
wrapped her legs around him, he felt her cold belt-buckle
between their stomachs and watched as one of the old
women calmly unwound the bandage layer by layer, it was
apparently a simple strip of adhesive, a type of insulating
tape. While the pig, which was now squealing loudly and
urinating, either from fear or pain, jerked about in vain
within the woman's grasp, a thin leg, which looked like a
stick compared to the rest of its body, appeared, eaten away
to the gleaming white bone in places by great festering sores.
After all three of them had regarded it for a while, one of
the old women went into the house and came out with a red
lacquered implement, looking something like a drill, a stun-
gun apparently. Iris, who could see nothing of all this from
the grass and assumed his lack of reaction was meant only to
spur her on, bit him in the chest and tried to get him moving
with a series of angry thrusts of her pelvis, he felt her hard
pubis. She raked her fingernails across his back and finally
struck the inside of his elbows with the edge of her hands so
that he fell upon her with his whole weight, and joined in
her rhythm. In spite of her breath in his ear, her breathless
whispers, he could not fail to hear the small round noise in
the farmyard below, it wandered on behind his closed eyes
as a black dot. He raised his perspiring face above the

woman who was now moaning, biting the backs of her hands, twisting her legs, and saw the dead animal, the old women at work on it with long, narrow blades, while the child carried a bowl of blood into the house.

Later, when Iris noticed the split body of the pig on the white wall—the neighbor's dogs surrounded the courtyard, their noses lifted, sniffing—he told her what he had seen. She frowned, shook her head, and he, who in spite of his desire felt that he had somehow been violated, strengthened himself now through her horrified reaction. Word by word he dragged the pig once more toward the steaming tub and removed the wrapping from its rotting leg. Yet after the first few sentences she seemed to have stopped listening. It's absolutely wrong, she said, with an expert knowledge that seemed to him shocking, absolutely wrong to drag an animal by force to the place where it's to be slaughtered. The fear of death not only upsets its circulation but also its hormonal balance and fills its flesh with toxic substances, so that the taste and smell of the meat is spoiled. You have to lure the animal carefully, talk nicely to it, with a carrot, a little clover. What's the problem, she said, as he showed his disgust. I suppose you don't eat meat?

*

They spent a few more hours in Florence before returning to Germany. As usual, the city was filled with tourists who made a point of ignoring each other, as self-conscious as customers at a brothel. A waitress from Lauter's café stepped out of a boutique and smiled at Iris. A double-decker tourist bus, its motor racing, was hung up in one of the narrow side streets, several of which already lay in evening shadows, while high above, beneath the afternoon blue of the sky, the tin roofs were gleaming. It was Saturday, several shiny limousines decorated with flowers were parked in front of various churches, from a high-arched dark portal flickered the crackling lights of countless flash bulbs. Iris was wearing a necklace of large green plastic beads, a light gray, knee-length, shapeless dress, and green shoes. She walked a few steps in front of him balancing herself on the curb with outstretched arms, and whenever the sun shone from one of the side streets through the material of her dress, he could see the outline of her body. No doubt sensing his desire, she turned around and smiled hesitantly at him. The tenderness with which he embraced her, his unexpected ability to do so, seemed even to him like a caress—from somewhere. It was tenderness enough for two. He saw with astonishment that Iris was crying. I don't know, she replied to his question, suddenly I feel so small and strong.

The train was crowded, and he stood in the aisle most of the way to Munich. At one point a place was free in a compartment and Iris, who was comfortably situated on an emergency seat, pointed him toward it. But he didn't want to go in, he didn't like the sort of people he knew were inside. They were typical German tourists, drinking beer and brandy, and calling Italians foreigners even in Verona. As far as he could hear, they conversed almost entirely in bald assertions. The man is worthless as a coach; they're taking the money from *our* pockets; you're only as old as you smell. All citrus drinks were Fanta to them, paper tissues were Tempos, and when one of them wanted to know the time, he asked the other what his Rolex said. But Assen was surprised to hear in this rattle of speech-chips the words *perhaps, possibly,* and *maybe*—even if it was only about the local team's chances to move up in the rankings. So doubt was still possible. Now I know, he said to Iris, what distinguishes Germans from the Germans.

The chrome reflected the morning sun in a fine spray. Still in pajamas, the landlord was tightening a screw on his mo-ped and didn't look up as Assen entered the front hall of the building. The mailbox was stuffed with ads. He leafed through a few letters and went up the stairs without a word.

An invitation to a poetry reading reminded him of a recurring dream: he's standing before the audience; a woman in a dress with a military cut has said a few words about him by way of introduction, and he's looking through a folder for some poems to read. But all he finds are drafts, coffee-stained notes, a few hastily scribbled half-formed thoughts, a typescript so heavily corrected it's illegible. He can't believe his eyes and leafs through everything once again. The audience, after a minute or so of expectant silence, starts to get restless. Whispering, coughing, scraping their feet—he's sure that the texts are in the folder, and yet he doesn't look up to say a few words of apology, to ask them to be patient. He's sweating beneath the spotlight shining down from the upper reaches of the cupola, which follows every hesitant step he takes to escape it. He forces himself to breathe deeply and goes through the thick pile one more time, page by page; it keeps slipping through his nervous fingers, fanning out like a big deck of cards, flapping back and forth. From the corners of his eyes he sees the flare of individual matches, the smell of smoke creeps toward him, he can hardly keep the pile together. Since there's no place he can set it down, he kneels and places it comfortably on his left thigh, with his leg out at an angle, so that he can go on leafing through it. He searches in vain, it's as if the poems were never written, what he has with him is simply unreadable. He stands up (a few pages flutter down onto the stage) and lifts his head expecting looks of impatient scorn. Yet the members of the audience, those who haven't already left at any rate—he had assumed the scraping chairs and the repeated creak of the doors were the sounds of more people coming—seem to have long since forgotten about him. There are great gaps in the hall; people are whispering to each other across empty rows, a woman is reading a newspaper, two men are baring their teeth for each other, showing off their new gold crowns. Just a moment, please, he calls out in shock, and slips past the angry stare of the woman organizer back to the cloakroom, where he quickly goes through his coat pockets. But there aren't any poems there either. Now he decides to recite the poems by heart, to keep more people from leaving he declaims the first line into the hall while he's still in the cloakroom. A few members of the audience who had already risen take their seats again, others break off their conversation. When he finds himself beneath the spotlight again he can't remember how the second line goes. The last of his listeners leave the hall, shaking their heads, the woman in charge turns out the lights, and he stamps his feet in the dark as if that will bring the words back to him, keeps stamping his feet until he has stripped the bed covers from his body and wakes up shivering.

*

Lauter was sitting at one of his cloth-covered tables, a portable typewriter beside a bottle of wine. The café was almost empty. A few young people dressed like members of some sect were ignored so long by the waiter that they finally left. We don't serve people in uniform, Lauter said. Not long ago they were all apocalyptic pessimists enraptured with the end of the world, now they're all enlightened. And when you ask them what they're enlightened about they can't explain it in words. They have a way of not talking that makes you look stupid for talking. Trying to express things is our form of cancer. But maybe I just don't like them because they spend so little money, all those tea drinkers. — He jerked a blank page from the typewriter and wadded it up. I've got to try to keep calm. If you've got to have something to say to be a writer, I'm up creek without a paddle. The moment I find a striking phrase, it strikes me dumb, and when I call a spade a spade, it's usually a shovel. My notes are bursting with ideas that go bust at a second reading, cerebral carpet fringe, intellectual daisy-chains. I get totally lost in the labyrinth of my thoughts, and can't produce one simple sentence. One old guy, a good cus-

tomer, said to me the other day, write about your generation, tell me what moves them, what paralyzes them, that
whole video brood. Sure, I said to him, could you give me
my generation's phone number? Someone like that's always
talking about making an impression; he wants to make an
impression with his work. When I suggested he ought to
learn to operate a ditch-digger if he wanted to make a deep
impression he walked out of the bar without a word. If my
imagination functions at all anymore, it daydreams about
royalties. And the hard thing isn't wrestling with my lack of
imagination, it's trying to keep from becoming moralistic
because of it. As the scales fall from my eyes I find myself
becoming more and more critical of others. I always used to
be afraid that I wasn't totally on top of things—even if it was
only so that I could look down on others. But now I know
that being on top of things *is* this fear itself. And I also know
that the top isn't much, and I don't worry about it anymore.
I stare for hours in one direction, without finding my
direction. The sun sets behind my typewriter and shines
through a blank page. A Sylvia comes to mind, I cross her
out, ditto for Karin. I try to get hold of an idea and wind up
with my prick in my hand. By that time I finally realize I'd
rather be with a woman. But when I'm with a woman, I can't
write anymore, then I've become a couple. And what could
be more wretched, more ridiculous, more hopeless than a
couple? Each one a small idyllic village to itself. They've
barely entered into a relationship, the stragglers, when the
relationship begins to destroy them, and you watch as each
of them withers in the shadow of the other. Because they're
taken care of and don't have to win anyone over, they lose all

their winning qualities, including their imagination. Each of them becomes an instrument for the frictionless fulfillment of the other's desires, so much of one mind you can't tell them apart. They talk to one another so long that in the end there's nothing left to hide, except the occasional whiskey bottle in the broom closet. Where was I? Talking about writing. Or the woman from the bakery gets out of her car, breasts like loaves of bread, which promptly provokes a typo. It's clear I'm dreaming about giving her a thorough kneading some day. She smiles, we press our dough-colored bodies together in spirit, and I slip in my cherry stem until I get hungry and let her husband palm off day-old pastries on me. And between the lines the roar of the traffic. To write freehand, another dream I once had. But my mind is crumpled by the demands of the paper, there's nothing left in my hands after days of slogging away but six or seven sentences that squirm in empty ambiguity like earthworms in marmalade. More and more often I get the feeling I'm being backed up against the wall by the difficulty of writing, about to be shot by my own text.

*

Iris didn't call for a long time; a bit hurt, Assen dialed her number. She picked up the phone and took a bite from an apple before answering. In his bad mood her voice seemed brighter than normal, almost glittering. —Yes, no, she couldn't get together with him right now, she had so terribly many deadlines. And her sister was due to arrive from Hamburg at any moment. She described the seasonings of a dinner in great detail, but didn't invite him to it. As if there were nothing of any greater importance between them, she told him about a borrowed sewing machine and a broken shoe. —What's the matter, she said after a while, don't just sit there saying nothing, like I owe you some explanation. Startled, he begged her pardon, but continued to say nothing. He'd planned on spending the evening with her, but now, in his disappointment, anything he said would sound artificial, or worse yet polite. He was relieved when she laid the phone aside with a quick "hold on a minute," spoken almost past the receiver, and puttered about in the kitchen, cursing, but constantly whistling a tune between curses. The trill of a steam kettle slowly faded away, a pot lid fell to the floor and rattled around and around for a long time. Later she wanted to know how he was doing, and while he talked she softly hummed a melody along with the radio. By the time they were finished they'd had a telephone conversation.

*

Even though the trip had been brief, it had been enough to render the city pleasantly foreign, to move it a thought away from him, giving him living space for a few days. That the city had changed while he was away because he was away was a thought which made him feel more at home than did the city itself. It was too easy to think of himself as living somewhere else to feel at home here. Berlin, the Cloud-Cuckoo-Land of state-supported culture-vultures, a cardboard city built on dog shit, as Lauter called it, had long since ceased to excite him. Above all, as subject matter.

Artificial grass. In the "West World" department store he talked with a salesgirl who had just immigrated from the East. There were more things to buy, she said, but in human terms she thought things were really lousy. —In what way, Assen asked. —Oh, the way everyone thinks of only one thing, and always in German currency. The only place you hear the words love or friendship, for example, are over a microphone. Everything's set to music. Everyone wants to jump straight into bed, with no personal commitment. The city seems to me an overblown case of venereal disease. And even so, eveyone keeps to themselves, even when they're with other people. Each person stares out of his own precious personality as if from the bottom of a well. There aren't any real human beings anymore, just night people. And in the morning you don't even get breakfast.

But Assen was also thankful to this dump of a city for its shadowy character, its colorful disorder, which had gradually opened his eyes to the false security of all ways of life. He had always known he was alone, but here he experienced it physically for the first time. In any case it was a good place to be somewhere else in your thoughts. In Berlin, where many things found expression more quickly than the truth allowed, he saw himself mounted like a cartoon figure in a realistic film—there was a thin layer of air between the soles of his shoes and the asphalt, and sometimes he asked himself if all suffering in this traceless presence weren't simply a convention, a phantom pain, like a disabled person feels in a leg long since amputated.

*

Attacks of jealousy: to feel himself absent. As if his blood turned bitter from one moment to the next: to feel himself absent. From her side.

*

Several police vans were parked on the sidewalk in front of the railway station, officers in battle dress sat on the running boards reading newspapers. Someone had drawn an exclamation mark behind the word "police" on one of the cars. Above the zoological gardens, the sunlight dissolved in a yellow-gray haze; three bums were sleeping in a recess in the wall. Sitting crowded together, leaning against one another, they reminded him of photos of dead soldiers in foxholes on the front line. A car door slammed and a swarm of pigeons flew up in front of the subway entrance where a woman was standing. She was carrying a small attaché case and wore red patent-leather high-heeled shoes and a dark gray pin-striped suit. Her pretty face looked tired, still not quite right in its perfection, which would awaken fear punctually with the opening of business. Assen was moved by the way she stood motionless on the last step but one of the stairway opening, gazing out with annoyance at the station square. The creaking doors of the entrance, the passengers hurrying by, tapping folded morning papers on their thighs, the passing taxis squealing their brakes—this was obviously not her world. She looked like someone who held an important position, and he figured her car must be in the shop at the moment. He grinned and hoped he'd never find himself in front of her desk requesting something of vital importance, he imagined her listening to him,

bored, while she regarded her multiple image in the mirrors
of her polished fingernails. You know what your problem
is? she'd ask, and continue without pausing: Your problem
is . . . She looked at her watch. Pushing her red hair back
with her hand, she walked toward the railway station, her
heels clicking. The policemen whistled, she gave a brief
smile, but didn't let it bother her as she went her way, which
would surely lead, thought Assen, toward success, to the
peak of a career, bypassing her sexuality.

Across the empty parking lot where he was waiting in his
taxi, across the maze of painted lines for parking spaces,
flitted a few dry linden leaves, driven like tiny wheels by the
wind, like the little cogged wheel with a wooden handle his
mother used long ago to perforate her dress patterns. And
then he remembered the suits she once made for his brother
and him, the same color as the pin-striped suit of the woman
who had just disappeared into the station. For one whole
summer these ridiculous creations tortured them every
Sunday. The outfit consisted of a vest they had to wear with
a white shirt, and short pants without a section for the fly,
since that was supposedly too hard to make. In its place a
seam ran straight down from the navel, digging into their
genitals. Assen remembered the hot tears he held back
when his playmates (who were almost all wearing long pants
by then) once yelled at them: Here come the splitniks.

If they took a "Sunday walk," their mother would wear
her dress of the same material. Striding along behind them,
she kept telling them not to "shamble" (did they want people
to think they were gypsies?), to follow the line of the pavement blocks. And she would punctuate her orders with

corrective blows from her purse or umbrella. Assen, already ashamed at being reprimanded in front of others, held himself so straight in his panic that he was hectored from behind not to walk in such an unnaturally stiff way.

*

The longer Iris went without contacting him, the more he was tortured by the thought that she was withdrawing. And this feeling could not be thought away, or slept away, or washed down with a beer; on the contrary. All the while he was trying to talk himself out of it—there was after all no reason why she should drop him—it etched itself ever more deeply into his mind. Evidence, he thought, though he knew he would be unlikely to believe it anyway. (That he had doubts at all seemed evidence enough to him.) With every day that she didn't call, he felt increasingly deprived of her attention, like an imaginary set of scales on which he would one day no longer rise: more clearly than himself he felt the weight of another person.

He thought immediately of the motorcyclist, of her smile reflected in his visor.

*

No question about it, he had missed a few signs, a nuance in her silence, a pointed civility, a raised brow. He was ashamed about this, since he often prided himself secretly on his sensitivity, which she had referred to more than once as misplaced, because he only applied it to himself. He realized with a shock that Iris could now count on him, that the invigorating struggle over the degree of their closeness, that stimulating doubt which kept them alive to each other, had disappeared. They understood one another so well that there no longer had to be understanding, they crawled to each other like sluggish fur-bearing animals, sleeping through questions until they no longer cared about the answers.

*

Keep cool. Iris must have things to do, seminars, exams, her sister, everything would clear up before long. His anxiety caused him to live faster than the passing time. But he didn't want to call her again, because according to an unstated but carefully observed rule it was Iris's turn. It was ridiculous. But now it was important. He forced himself to work. At his desk, in a state of absent-minded concentration, he managed to bear up temporarily.

*

It seemed like some form of mockery visited upon him that this woman, whom he had grown to know so well in the meantime, was now turning into a mystery again before his eyes. He could have lived without her very well, as long as he could be sure that she wanted him. But her supposed defection tore him from his own unsensed element, disturbed his chaos. Yesterday's circumspect pedestrian now stumbled along, an accident waiting to happen. A truck-driver leaned back and jammed on the brakes, his load capsizing beneath the canvas. He brushed against a shoe salesman, sending a pile of boxes tumbling in front of a fruit stand. Stammering his apologies, Assen gathered them up while the man stood silently looking on, his arms folded over his chest. A woman in a loose satin blouse, through which he could see the nipples, stuck her tongue out at him. People loaded down with packages emerged through the automatic glass doors of department stores, looking about for the next thing they could buy, their faces devoid of all expression but the compulsion to shop. He was consoled by the fact that every one of them seemed to suffer from some sort of pathological condition: a weak heart, poor circulation, greed; to make himself feel better at their expense, he dismissed them all as cripples. It was impossible to imagine any delicacy of feeling behind such faces. Hate-twisted faces, he thought, and saw in the next instant, in the mirror of a shop window, his own face, twisted by hate.

*

If he had found happiness with her thus far, then it was a darkness within, as the inner darkness of a gold nugget. What more did their relationship mean to him than proof that he could win a beautiful woman. This fact often satisfied him more lastingly than did Iris, that beautiful woman. With the best of wills, he could not say he loved her, or had ever loved her, unless he had a false conception of love. Wasn't it wrong even to try to conceive of love? Did he shrink from the feeling because his notion of it still drew upon a few isolated moments in puberty? He sensed that it would no longer come from a clear blue sky, that it had to be worked for, lovingly. But that was a truth too uncomfortable not to continually slide into oblivion. Lauter, leathery Lauter, had called out: You're in love, man. He himself felt nothing (or at most disgust at the defiant declaration that he no longer felt anything).

*

That he even thought about another person: was that not already the shadow of its shadow? That from now on he would seek signs in her gestures, in her face: was that not already its sign?

*

He forgot to turn off the faucet, or to flush the toilet. He stumbled over garbage bags he'd put out in the hall to empty later, mashing bits of food, tea leaves, and eggshells on the hallway rug. He no longer washed, he slept in his clothes. His apartment smelled of stale flower water. On his desk stood a little dish of mashed potatoes studded with cigarette butts. By late morning he would be drunk, popping Valium, and staring for hours on end at the soundless flicker of the TV screen. After a few days his teeth were so thickly coated he could scrape them with a fingernail. He remembered the kettle on the gas stove long after it was glowing hot. He didn't notice that he'd left the refrigerator door wide open until the clumps of ice beneath the freezer section clattered to the kitchen floor.

He worried that something might be wrong with his phone and he couldn't be reached, so he called Lauter and asked him to call back. The telephone was working.

On his pillow he found the hairline impressions of her eyelash mascara. He poured whiskey in his wine and thought about the other man, who seemed more and more obtrusive in his absence, and whom he could only conceive of as his opposite. He was the stick-in-the-mud, the other guy rode a motorcycle. He was the plank in her bed, the other was a dream: the other guy's life smelled of peppermint and was just too good to be true. He just got a little drunk once in a while, after passing an exam, say, and checked his watch before he had his last drink. Whatever he hadn't experienced he could easily imagine. Life was like an office where he felt at home. A guy like that knew what he wanted, he wasn't always cutting himself with sharp, clumsy thoughts. He'll get his cut of life, Iris my dear. He'll give you a family over the abyss, he'll build you a house on top of the nuclear stockpile, he'll come up with your wretched rent.

*

In another life he would kill him.

*

It had rained all night, a giant's hand constantly crumpling silk paper outside his window. The morning-gray cooing of the doves, claws scrabbling on the windowsill. Cars starting up here and there, the windowpanes vibrating, tickling his nose. He'd been awake a long time, staring at the overcast sky. He felt irritated from head to toe; he moved his tongue carefully in his mouth; his teeth felt jagged, like broken fragments. When he yawned his lips cracked. As if in scorn, like a wooden laugh, a truck rumbled over ridged asphalt, a mo-ped revved its engine. Roller-doors rattled up. He pulled the covers over his head. Through the wall socket by his bed he could hear a faint voice singing on the radio.

Oh, Assen. In the end he'd been vain enough to talk himself into a passion, he'd fanned a breath of pain into a bonfire. In the end he stared from the stubble of his face like a tomcat in a thunderstorm. Still it was some consolation that "the other man" was something more than an *ideé fixe,* that he possessed a certain corporeality, even though, like the flesh of ghosts, he found it hard to envision. No doubt he felt him so clearly only because he was a part of himself: Iris wrote from Hamburg, where her sister's husband, who was a doctor, had his practice, to tell him she was pregnant. And happy. See you soon.

He read Rudolf Borchardt's novel *United by a Common Enemy* for a second time. It was one o'clock in the morning when he heard steps on the stairway, heavy boots, men's voices, a metallic clatter. He forced himself to finish reading the paragraph before he went to look. "I will not allow myself," the sentence read, "to ask more of circumstances than the bare necessities and this room." It seemed to him a beautiful, luxurious sentence, and he copied it down in his notebook. As he stepped from his living room into the dark entrance hall, the gleam of a flashlight struck him in the face—through the mail slot in his apartment door. The beam moved over him calmly, down his right and left pant leg, over his hands, and back to his face again. —What do you want, he asked into the glare, and was answered by a voice that seemed born to keep everything and everyone in order. The fact that it was the police did not relieve him greatly. He opened the door.

There's been an accident in the apartment, one of the three uniformed men said, and stepped inside. May we come in. The others walked past him and disappeared inside with their crackling radios. Assen thought he must have misheard the policeman. An accident in the apartment, he said again in repetition of his opening assertion, and began to check the kitchen. But no one's had an accident here, said Assen. (Something fell to the floor in the next room and one of the men laughed.) We'll see about that, said the officer. He made a point of ignoring the disarray in the room, its most striking feature. He gave the impression he was seeking something more substantive, presumably the underlying principle behind it. At the same time he tried to look bored, as if everything were normal, nothing to be alarmed about. He chewed his gum slowly, with his mouth closed.

The others came back, one of them waggled his finger negatively. —You're right, said the one apparently in charge, smiling now. No accident here. Well, no harm done—probably a misunderstanding at the head office. That happens sometimes. Now if you're the registered occupant of this apartment, everything's in order. —Of course I am! —Of course, the officer said. Can I see your I.D. And Assen showed him his I.D. in his own kitchen. They claimed not to know who had called in the alarm, but they wished him a good night. As he locked his door—using

the safety bolt as well for the first time—he had the feeling
that he was sealing off something long since contaminated.

*

The next morning he cleaned up his apartment, took a
bath and shaved, and then decided to go to a café.

To have a child with Iris, to be locked into a decades-long
responsibility by her—nothing since he had been called up
for military service seemed more threatening. If in spite of
this he sometimes asked himself why not, it was simply to
avoid future difficulties with her by not allowing them to
arise, at least in his mind. Given how unintentionally, how
casually, the little grub had come into being, he had no
desire to grant it value or dignity; a biological slip-up, an
outgrowth of their heated nonrelationship, the removal of
which was merely a technical matter: consultations, forms to
be filled out, running about. And yet he was astonished to
find that he kept feeling the child physically, as if it were
growing not only in Iris, but in some mysterious way within
himself as well. Or was he just being poetic again.

He reread her letter while filing his nails, her overly large,
domineering script. Several words ran off the edge of the
page and were simply repeated in the next line. Yesterday
he had grinned at the phrase: You've fathered a child. That
had a moving note of uncertainty about it, almost anxiety.
Now he banged his hand down on the page. So she already
sensed his defense. To outflank it she made of his sperm,
which in fact she'd always found a little repulsive, something
powerful, of real merit. Suddenly what she'd once sulkily

referred to as that "damn screwing" had become a creative act. She must really take him lightly. And she held her happy feeling under his nose like a swab of cotton wool doused in chloroform. No objections please. Second thoughts would only cloud her happiness. You might as well be a cannibal as have the heart to do such a thing. (When he thought about it more carefully, he realized that he was annoyed most of all by the fact that, like everybody else, she wrote "for you and I" instead of "for you and me.")

*

When he went to close his apartment door, he grasped only air. The landlord had unscrewed the doorknob. Of the doorbell too, nothing remained but two crooked wires sticking out of the plaster that sparked when they made contact. Assen kicked over a large bucket of white paint before he left the building. It flowed in silken waves down the steps into the basement, from which a curse soon arose, followed by splatting and thumping sounds as if the landlord were trying to run up the slippery stairs.

The pedestrian light turned red; butterflies, dead or in the throes of death, their wings jerking, lay scattered at intervals along the sidewalk. Children ran silently from one to the other, squashing them flat, like snowberries. At the window of a ground-level apartment, a man leaned staring into space, blinded by tears. Through the open entrance, Assen could see into the dark interior of a church; workers in blue uniforms were welding something on a crucifix. A single bell rang out as if by error in the noon heat, emphasizing the stillness of the street he now crossed, the light still red.

On the other side a woman was waiting beside a baby carriage stuffed with a thick, puffy eiderdown. Her eyes lay deep in the shadow of her beetling brow and yet he could see her angry gaze directed at him. —Young man, she said, although she was no older than he was, you're a fine example for the children. She pointed at the traffic light. — Who're you talking to, he replied as he walked on. And was already past her when she yelled: Someone should give you a good punch in the nose! Right in the face, you jerk! It was so shrill that a few neighbors jumped up behind the flowers of their balconies, and after craning their heads in annoyance in every possible direction, looked down silently at him as if he were some creature from another planet, now exposed as an outlaw.

He walked along stiffly, keeping close to the buildings, seriously expecting a blow, something thrown at him, hitting him in the small of the back, followed by a rain of other objects. He stepped through the sliding door of the café and almost stumbled over a small remote-controlled police car that a child was guiding around the tables. The waitress set an ashtray in front of him with a hello that sounded like a command to reply. He ordered coffee and a cognac, but then canceled the cognac. A woman selling newspapers table by table passed by his without stopping; he would have liked to ask her what she saw in his face. For a few moments he amused himself with the absurd notion that his hair had turned white during the preceding uproar. His folded hands clamped between his knees, he stared at his cup, in his mind he could still hear the woman upbraiding him. (Not that he had been bothered by her scolding; it was her voice, the sound of it, the nameless, bone-chilling, murderous, inhuman screeching of this nonperson that rendered him so thoroughly speechless. And he was angry with himself that his sense of hearing was so anxiously sensitive, that the tone in which words were spoken intimidated him more easily than the words themselves, that the sharp edge of a voice could make him lose his head.) He went to the bar and ordered a cognac after all.

*

He felt prepared by suggestion for what was to come. He saw young, tanned family fathers overseeing their loved ones, earnest and upright; yet the determined set of their faces had a helpless cast. He saw women relaxing in their inaccessibility, growing fatter and fatter, children launched into childhood, choking the family dog beneath the table. That was the normal course of things, a brief stirring, the first tax bracket, then a long twilight in the next two or three. Herr Hölderlin, booth four please.

He had a job once with the post office, carrying packages to the suburbs during the Christmas season, through mushy snow, deep into darkening afternoons. Melted water and vomit on the artificial stone steps, elevator buttons scorched by stubbed-out cigarettes, noisy stereos, and standing in each of a thousand doors the same frowning lord of the manor, the same child-restraining wife in the background, the same sounds from the TV—now he knew it all. And yet he found it hard to believe. That these people didn't object to the way they lived, *were* the way they lived, the slightest blow would destroy them. Nor could he criticize them, try as he might, he simply became weaker day by day, and finally fell ill. (Prestressed concrete: a fever word; coughs, echoing like a hundred stairwells.) Not that he was anything but normal in his more or less compassionate distance. Presumably he differed only in the anger he felt at not being different.

*

Someone at the next table asked him what time it was. A time of animals he murmured, the hair on his arms felt apelike. What did he have in mind when he thought of himself as a man, crouching over his scrotum, with his sperm. Nothing of course. He'd never worried about his maleness, he thought only of the charm all women shared— and found it shocking to discover all at once that it supposedly had a purpose; up to then it was its very pointlessness that had seemed to him so sensible. And his "image" of women (he thought of the word as if it described a type of pain) hardly differed from that on the TV screen or in the tabloids. He accepted his allegiance to these commercial conceptions of beauty as a negative but nevertheless human characteristic: something forgivable. What he'd met of the female sex thus far, motorcycle queens and disco birds, career women and budding schoolteachers, sex bombs and feminists, seemed impossible to relate to a fertile womb. Blinded by a smile or by his longing for it, he never perceived the person beneath the rouge, nor the womb beneath the lace panties. When he asked what sort of birth control she was using (he took it for granted that *she* would handle that side of things) Iris had simply replied, Oh, I'm sucking peppermints. How 'bout you? He assumed she was uncomfortable talking about such technical matters, and trusting her to take the necessary precautions, he dropped the subject.

Now he saw children in the park across the way; he watched them yanking up flowers with a lasso.

*

Duped by all the love stories in the world, he suddenly discovered in the face of every woman a gentle, more or less cosmetically concealed, maternal instinct—or at least a tendency in that direction. The black blouse of the waitress had a wet spot about breast level, he immediately saw it as overflowing milk. Every time he looked out the window he saw pregnant women walking proudly by. Lost in their thoughts, they smiled as if relieved that they no longer had to pretend to their own personalities: at last they could just be mothers. He read in their faces a disturbing self-satisfaction, a sense of triumph that along with the baby they'd presumably been waiting for so long, they would now have their husbands as well: pinned down to house and home. The men meanwhile seemed disgustingly docile, spineless, impotent workers employed by their own erections, caught unawares by a law of nature they had overlooked in their world of legal sections and paragraphs. And suddenly, with no scruples about stereotyping them (at the moment he couldn't conceive of them as individuals), he only wanted to curse the whole of the female race: their permanent-wave brains, their stupid flower faces. Their firm belief that they were better beings, with a higher sense of morality, their silent domineering attitude, no matter where they went, their self-certainty, as if each swing of their hips moved the world—spare me please! They weren't worth the pain of squeezing out a single love poem, these paper-curlers, every symphony was lost on those ears deafened by squawling babies, every picture was painted in the sand before those dull maternal eyes. Can you name, he asked himself, a *single* totalitarian regime, past or present, in which *women* organized the resistance or ran it? Characterless, like water seeking its level, the main thing was to have a belly full of babies. Attach a baby to each breast and life is always worth living, even in the worst tangle of barbed wire. Just so they'll be loved, so they won't be alone for a single moment, they pop out one kid after the other onto this pitiful planet; leave them alone for a second and they collapse like robots with the power cut off. And why can't they seem to do anything in science and art, these airheads, for instance why don't women ever start up a religion? Because they have about as much sense for metaphysics as cows have for national public radio. Only when they've grown old and the children have left home do they darken the interiors of churches with their black dresses and remind their god in prayer to be sure and put on his winter underwear.

After downing his next cognac he started to feel that he was wise to all their tricks, but he would keep it to himself. His head lowered, he watched them like someone who knew more than was good for him. He made a point of making himself inconspicuous, that is, he continued to stare as always at his favorite spots. And indeed from the way they preened and postured, the way they shimmered beneath his melancholy gaze, it seemed the women just couldn't imagine that anyone would find them anything other than desirable: witches in the form of angels, who wished to drive him into the darkness, drive him to drink with their hips, to a hell of hearth and home. Each lowering of their eyelids was suddenly a sign of it, each smile, each gesture seemed aimed only at the child in the man. Their gentleness now struck him as babying, their beauty as a catalyst for his seed. He was the water boy of creation. They blossomed.

Holy simplicity. His ideas probably weren't even dumb. He was probably too naive to be dumb.

*

Two days later Iris called. She must have been sitting at an open window, he could hear church bells. She said, Hi, it's me, and then fell silent. —How are you, he asked, and was instantly annoyed by his meek tone. Are you in pain? Of course she would turn this silly question against him immediately, so he laughed to neutralize it. —What's that, she asked, what did you say, I can't understand a word. —How are you, he repeated loudly enough to drown out the Sunday sounds at the other end, and was irritated by his own shouting. Did she want to entrench herself in noise? —Wait a minute, she said, then the bells sounded as if they were behind glass. —Now what was it you said? I burned a cake and had to air things out. When he asked his question for the third time it sounded gentle in spite of himself, almost tender. —I'm not doing so well, she said, my stomach hurts, I upchucked this morning. —Up-what? —Upchucked! — What's that, he said, although of course he knew. But he wasn't about to let her talk baby talk with him. —Good god, Iris cried, upchuck is upchuck, any kid knows that! I'm not as uptight about words as you are!

They laughed, for much too long. Then, as she launched into a detailed description of Hamburg, her sister's apartment, and her brother-in-law's new practice, he broke in to ask when they were going to see each other again. She was silent for a few heartbeats, during which he forgot to breathe, and then she said quietly: Not just now. —And why not? —I don't know. I'm sorry. —You don't know? —I can't tell you why, it's too silly. Don't be angry. —What's silly? — Stop asking questions. You'll just laugh if I tell you. —Try me. —It's too silly. I'm afraid. —Of what? —You'll think I'm crazy. —Why? —Please, promise me you won't think I'm crazy or something, ok? She paused. You could tell by the silence that she was close to tears. —I'm just afraid, she swallowed hard, I'm afraid you'll do away with the baby. It's stupid, I know, I can't explain it myself. —Do away with the baby? —Well, not surgically or anything like that, I know that. But with your presence; as if everything would be extinguished inside me, darkened, or somehow bewitched if I were around you. But like I said, I know how silly that is. I guess I'm just hysterical. I'm sorry.

He pursed his lips in a soundless whistle, as if he were sneaking away. He saw his image reflected on the blank TV screen and couldn't read anything in his face. He noticed a pigeon on the windowsill, its eye orange, in the kitchen a drop of water fell from the faucet with the bright echoing sound he knew from films about caves. Iris took a deep breath and released it in a rush of relief. He lit the filtered end of a cigarette.

Not that her tears would have rendered him helpless (he wasn't worried about helping her). But he felt himself turning soft and compliant in the face of wishes she had not yet uttered, and which were more likely to be demands than requests. And like a man who sees himself still falling in a dream before he jerks himself awake to safety, it was not until she sighed again on the other end that he realized his soft compliance was setting a fate in motion contrary to all his logical impulses and instincts, before which he could only bury his face in his hands.

That's all right, he said, lost in thought, you're not hysterical, calm down—and heard her in high spirits, almost babbling, launching into new stories of Hamburg, her brother-in-law's hobbies, and her sister's children, who had discovered that butterflies stink. And when he asked again cautiously when they might meet, her reply was already less vague, as if her fear had dissolved with her tears. But she didn't want to get together before the end of next week, because she was moving: into a commune, student friends of hers, pure chance. By chance a room was free, on the sunny side, fourth floor.

*

The cough of a repairman echoed through the gas line, a rusty stream flowed from the faucet. A drill howled beneath his rooms, then whirred dully as it entered the plaster. Chalk dust trickled quietly from old nail holes in the wall, like sand in an hourglass.

Something hit the tin window ledge with a bang. Looking down he saw the landlord shading his eyes with both hands, staring upward. He had apparently thrown a rock. Assen laughed soundlessly behind the window. The other man pressed his lips together, scraped around with his foot in the sand among the empty bags of concrete, and found another rock that he hefted threateningly. Assen pulled his shirt open at the chest, but still stepped aside when the half brick came flying at him, whirling on its axis. It hit the side of the building just below his window. He opened it and sat on the sill. —That one's too big, you're losing your cool. Grab a smaller one. It's not the size but the speed that counts. With the right type of gun you could be killed with your own shirt button. Step back a little, the angle's throwing you off. You'll get hit on the head when it comes back down. And remember to figure in the height as well as the distance: your perspective's distorted. Aim a bit above me if you really want to hit me.

It won't be long, wiseass, yelled the landlord, and threw a third missile, a chunk of plaster. Assen could tell immediately that it was going to fall short, and just sat there with his arms crossed. The landlord, his mouth open, followed the flight of the chunk with slowly rising eyebrows, as if he wanted to lift the arc higher, the high arc which carried it through the brand-new "studio" window on the third floor and on into the apartment, rattling across the freshly varnished parquet floor. The landlord grabbed his head in both hands, as if it had clattered through his own skull.

I told you so, Assen yelled down, and waggled his finger. You're not as strong as you think. You'll only hurt yourself; live by the gun, die by the gun. Relax, stay cool, remember your ulcers. I think I see a smaller rock over there to the left. The other man shook his head as if emerging from a daydream and looked around wildly for something to throw. Growling through his teeth, he hurled a fourth chunk—which once more merely flew through the now empty windowframe below. It clattered on the wood floor in pure mockery.

Assen couldn't watch any longer. He took his steam iron from the bookcase and lifted it slowly in the sunlight before the other's staring eyes. Then—as the landlord turned his head, shielding it with raised hands, which made him appear somehow delighted—he gave a cry and knocked out the window with two or three quick blows. It was already cracked anyway.

*

The building Iris now lived in was open, the stairwell smelled of whiskey. Assen felt she was barricading herself from him in the commune, nesting within a circle of friends who of course were all "for" the baby, as she told him on the phone. It was like entering enemy territory when she opened the door. He peered skeptically over her shoulder into the interior of the apartment, greeted by the thumping drone of a washing machine. Iris led him in by the wrist.

At the end of the long hall, in a bright rectangle of light which fell through the window onto the coco runner, surrounded by all kinds of children's toys, stood a dish of grapes impaled by needles. In one of the open rooms he saw a cat sleeping in a baby cot. No one else was home, and because Iris was still finding her own way about the apartment, going in the wrong door at one point, having trouble finding the tea kettle, the rooms lost their atmosphere of danger and turned neutral. They sat down at the kitchen table, their reversed reflections mirrored in its shiny brown surface, their foreheads nearly touching, like two playing cards lying side by side. —This blossoming in my stomach, Iris said, I can't eat a thing.

She didn't smile, there was even an affectionate resentment in her face, and at first Assen just wanted to look at her instead of talking—in her beauty she seemed to him to be right about everything. Everything within her that had turned outward, flickering nervously, was now at rest, she was radiant in a relaxed way, inwardly, as if filled by the reflection of all the blissful moments that lay ahead. The future no longer seemed doubtful, darkened by second thoughts, it had taken on physical form, a reason for joy, and the way she sat across from him, her hands lying open upon the table, expressed a gentle but unshakable confidence, physical strength, and a happy state of exhaustion. Her fingernails were unpainted, in fact she wore no makeup at all, and her hair was tied up as if she no longer needed to be admired. And even if the hint of a halo he saw above her head was nothing but a dreamy reflection of his affection, he viewed it with astonishment as something she had thus far hidden from him, like a final trump.

In her left ear she wore a ring he'd already noticed in Italy, an old, lusterless garnet he'd seen one morning while she was still asleep, lying on a book bound in white, emitting a mysterious spray of light, finer than the finest hair, in the milky dawn, shortly after which, right on cue, the first rays of the sun blazed up behind the wooded peak of Monte Albano.

Iris removed her rings and began rubbing cream on her hands. He was getting annoyed by the way she was lolling about, sitting there with her legs spread, as if she were several months along instead of a few weeks; the way she announced with her whole body that there was no point discussing it, the way she paraded her maternal majesty, in the shadow of which he was probably expected to feel like a butcher with his thoughts of abortion. No matter what they discussed, the way she inspected her fingernails or gazed at the ceiling let him know there was nothing she could do about it; she would listen without hearing; understand and not care. He narrowed his eyes in a flash of anger; so exaggerated that she imitated him. He quickly acted as if he had something in his eye.

He'd already called her a few times, contrary to their agreement, mostly when he was drunk, and after leading off with a few clumsy questions about how she felt, he would plead with her in a whining, wine-thickened voice not to bring a baby of his into the world, to stay out of his life story, not to turn him into a jackass pulling her baby buggy, and so on. Hurt by the absent-minded way she listened to him (she had her hands full with things to do in her new room) and by the calming tone in her voice, he would fall into cursing each time, yelling into the phone long after there was anyone there to hear him.

This time too she spoke in a gentle, calming tone. —Don't look at me like that, she said. You peer over your glasses like you're looking over the top of a crate. Don't creep inside yourself so. —She said he just didn't want to understand, that he was lying in wait behind his eyes for the chance to trip her up with his arguments (she emphasized the word *arguments*, as if they were some sort of crazy notions he had). She was thirty years old, she'd lived through plenty, and she would be more than happy to do without whatever she would miss in the future because of the baby. Why did he want to deprive her of an experience for which she had been placed in the world, perhaps the most meaningful experience of all, missing it would devastate her in the long run, she would fall ill, get pregnant with a tumor. —A tumor? Assen asked. —Breast cancer, or cancer of the womb, Iris said like the quick jab of a knife: the typical illness of childless women. After all, sexuality was not an end in itself, not some form of play at the close of day, and if he didn't want to have kids, why didn't he get himself sterilized? And his so-called objective reason for not having children, the bleak state of the world, was an empty one. There had always been catastrophes, earthquakes, wars, plagues, and people kept having children. Of course it wasn't logical, it was biological—the body had its own common sense, and she found that more convincing than his reservations, which were basically groundless. The fact was—and here she took a final puff on her cigarette and stubbed it out in the ashtray, breaking it in two—he wasn't really interested in what sort of life his child would have on this polluted planet. He would be just as happy wallowing in garbage or at war as long as he was left in peace, in his dreadful bookish peace, the eternal end of the world was just an easy excuse for him not to start anything new, he enjoyed living in misery, just as long as he could squeeze a poem or two out of the muck and everyone left him alone. Could he really share happiness with someone else, even have a family, given his egotism?

Assen lit her cigarette stub. His annoyance that she took it upon herself, without being asked, to form an image of him and discuss it with him was proof that it was at least partially accurate. In the face of this, he could think of nothing more effective than indignantly straightening his tie. And the more in the wrong he felt simply through his own silence, the more his remorse distorted Iris's voice, which finally sounded as if it were coming from behind a set of screens. He felt the hair prickle on the nape of his neck as he realized that what was speaking was the life force of a being who was already in another world.

In fact, said Iris, he was only afraid of the responsibility, of failing to live up to it. When he talked about his freedom he meant avoiding all obligations. But was it possible in the long run always to take from life and never give to it? And did he think that she, Iris, wasn't afraid of the future too, and the decades of responsibility, the burdens of motherhood? All that seemed like a great dark room before her—and yet she couldn't turn aside. (Something neither one of them were quite capable of understanding.) Yes, she was worried about taking this step—but didn't that just show it was the right one? A better world could only arise from better people, and *not* to grant this age a child seemed to her more brutal than the age itself.

She folded her arms across her chest and was apparently awaiting his reply—which only increased his defiance, the roaring emptiness inside him. The teacup was so fragile he wanted to shatter it. The dust on the windowpane glistened like silver in the sun. In the sink a pile of dishes shifted suddenly. The way out may be so obvious that I'm overlooking it, Assen thought. The shame of being cornered by her oppressed him so that he began to sweat. He felt a slight paralysis of his face, as if his stupidity was already taking on bodily form, he breathed shallowly, as in a faint. Any attempt to speak now would start off with a croak and make him appear totally ridiculous.

Iris followed the line of his gaze through the air, apparently surprised, given the situation, that he did nothing but look out the window. —We could go out for a little, she said.

*

She probably read his silence as an incipient acquiescence: on the street she took his arm and put her head on his shoulder, as if they could start making plans now. At the moment, however, Assen was neither for nor against the baby, he was most decidedly against himself, the way he walked along beside her, stiff and speechless, bumping against her soft body at every step, which he found annoyingly exciting. They walked along a sooty wall with bits of broken bottle gleaming on top, and then turned toward a cemetery; it *would* have to be a cemetery, he said. She was startled. She hadn't thought much about it; just that it was the only place with a few trees. The foliage of a long lane of chestnut trees cast flickering shadows on their bright clothes; Iris was wearing red shoes of translucent plastic, the soles of which—he was put off when he noticed it—left small heart-shaped imprints in the newly raked sand on the path. The cemetery was extensive and hilly, and at one point they looked down into a small valley filled with graves, whose golden inscriptions gleamed among the hedges. Then they found themselves once more beneath crosses angling up into the sky, walking beside almost perpendicular clay walls from which, as a jet broke the sound barrier above them, sand trickled, blown by tiny breezes. One grave was marked with a small sign: Plot rental due, Cemetery Administration. Beside the path stood a decaying bench, with waist-high stinging nettles growing through the wooden lathes of the seat. A single sandal in the grass, crushed beer cans, sun-bleached cigarette packs—here lie the outcasts, said Iris. They stopped in front of a small basin filled to the brim with water and watched the wriggling insects with amused disgust. As they stepped to the side, the sun's rays shot into the water like glassy knife blades.

She pointed out a gravestone that Assen noticed had been sprayed with a swastika: Sandra Hofer. Isn't Sandra a beautiful name? —For whom, he asked. She smiled blankly. Now he could look her cold-bloodedly in the eye again, he had the urge to punch her, because brats were apparently the only thing on her mind, even here, standing over the dead. At the same time it bothered him to catch her using such an obvious ploy, and in order not to shame her further, he looked away; and read the name Roderick on an old gravestone riddled with bullet holes. Roderick, he said aloud, simply surprised that such a name existed. —Oh, no, she said, not Roderick, it sounds like some robber baron. And she took his arm again, looking for other names.

*

He dreamed, as he often had recently, that he was to be shot. Iris carried her stomach like a kettledrum to the place of execution and beat out her happiness upon it. The shots were a blessing, three brief, clear snaps, and once he stuck his fingers in the bullet holes because he was ashamed of all the blood bubbling out. He always arose as if born anew and placed her hand upon her stomach, which was now flat. The crackling and humming of a long-distance line sounded in his voice when he said: I thought we'd never wake up.

*

Having said nothing more about the baby, Iris walked to the bus stop to wait with him. Leaning against a poster-board, she turned her face to the sun, humming. In spite of her beauty she seemed repellent to him now, a cheerful incarnation of the old adage about life going on in the face of death. He stared into a blocked-off hole in the sidewalk from which the smell of sewage arose along with radio music, a piano sonata. He imagined the water washing under the city cemeteries, peeling skeletons from the earth, carrying them along, millions of the dead, skulls and pelvic bones clashing together, rolling along, half-rotted cadavers, mice peering from the nostrils, an endless circular procession beneath the city's foundations, interrupted only now and then by a dead body thrown sideways by a rush of foamy, brownish-yellow sewage suddenly thundering out of a side tunnel. Then the bones pile up against each other, clacking and grinding, rising to the vaulted roof, until another rush of sewage comes from the other direction, tossing the rats into the air and breaking up the interlocking mass, and the river of feces and corpses, above which the great city sways in place, continues to circulate in almost total silence; nothing to be heard but a soft gurgling and bones clicking against one another—and even that only in the early morning hours, if you put your ear to the pipes in the bathroom.

Iris grabbed him by the shoulders and tugged at him until he lifted his head and looked her calmly in the eye. She took his right hand and placed it on her breast, then on her stomach. —Here, she said—and here: what do you think all this is for? I have the capacity, the strength, and the desire to bear children. Isn't it natural to go ahead and do it?

Now her look seemed angry, and he couldn't see himself reflected in her pupils. On her upper lip he noted incipient traces of the wrinkles she would have in old age. —Here, he said, and raised one fist and then the other. She didn't back off. I have the capacity, the strength, and sometimes even the desire, to beat someone to death. Would it be natural to go ahead and do it?

When he was already on the bus, as she looked up darkly at him, he saw two work gloves fly high into the air from the hole in the sewer behind her.

He could not and would not give him any information, the man on the telephone said, and it was clear from his voice that there was no use talking to him. There were counseling sessions every week—would he like to make an appointment? Of course there would be a small charge. — What are counseling sessions, Assen asked. —Sessions where you receive counseling. —But I don't need to be counseled, I just need some basic information, maybe some pamphlets, addresses . . . —We can't give that out without prior counseling, what do you think we're here for? And the addresses wouldn't do you any good anyway, they wouldn't let you in if you haven't been counseled. Just drop by sometime; it's painless and doesn't take long. —Fine, said Assen, I'll bring my I.D.

The health department had already closed, a cleaning woman unlocked the door. A few people waiting outside a glass door marked "Counseling Room" grunted or merely nodded when he said hello. He was surprised to see a woman there. She seemed to be caring for a man with a pigeon chest and thin legs who sat sleeping in a wheelchair. She had only one arm herself, with muscles like a body builder. The bare stump of the other arm extended from her short-sleeved T-shirt. The others included a young, almost juvenile man with his hair in a ponytail, and a person around forty with a mustache, cowboy boots, lederhosen, and a low-cut black sweater. A tiny gold knife dangling from a thin chain gleamed in the hair on his chest.

The door was opened promptly at seven o'clock by a young staff member wearing sandals and no socks. He looked out the window at the sky as he replied mechanically to the greetings of those entering. From the start, Assen felt threatened by the strained homeyness of the counseling room. They sat down on thinly padded steel chairs around a large circular table. There were pencils and index cards at each place, and everyone but Assen reached for them without being asked and started filling them in. Pencils only, please, the man called in from the next room, apparently a kitchen, from which, a moment later, he emerged with a tray laden with bottles of fruit juice and mineral water. The cards are machine-readable he added with a grin, looking around at the people writing and closing his eyes for just a moment when he reached Assen. I'm the state-approved psychologist here, he said, and winked as if that weren't so bad, then lowered himself into a chair. He suggested they all call each other by their first names, and that each of them introduce himself or herself and give a brief summary of his or her situation, so that they could all have an "exchange."

After a short silence the man with the mustache, in a loud voice intended to sound firm, said he was a computer programmer and had been married for ten years (happily you could say), had two children (silly but sweet little monkeys), and that at age forty-three his wife didn't want to have any more. But that wasn't so simple. Since he considered the traditional methods of contraception unreliable or potentially damaging to the health he'd decided on a vasectomy and had come for counseling about it. The psychologist nodded briefly, with the air of granting permission. It was now the turn of the man in the wheelchair, who tapped his wife, who scratched the stump of her arm in embarrassment before she began. They'd had four children altogether, the fifth one, last year, had been a miscarriage, and unfortunately there was now some danger of complications with pregnancy so that the doctor had advised them not to have any more. Since they didn't trust the regular methods, and an operation was much more complicated for a woman than a man, they'd decided to have him—she pointed at her husband—sterilized. (Assen noticed that he was already asleep again.) The young man, who kept winding a strand of his hair around his index finger and jiggling his leg up and down, was training to be a nurse. He was eighteen years old, had a lot of girlfriends, and wanted to be sterilized so that they could fuck without having to worry about it anymore. The woman pushed her glasses back in place, covering her face with her hand, the man with a mustache grinned. —Did he have any children, the psychologist asked. —No, was that a requirement? He didn't want any, it would be stupid, what with the acid rain and all, there were already enough mutants around. —And the traditional methods, had he already tried them with his girlfriends? —Of course, he'd tried them all. The whole business was a pain and disgusting and unerotic. —The diaphragm too? Confused silence. And smiling smugly, as if he'd suspected it all along, the psychologist looked around the circle. —Did he know what a diaphragm was? —Yes, he thought so, but he couldn't exactly . . . At any rate he wanted to be sterilized, bang, so he could forget about the whole business. Now the psychologist reached behind him to a bookshelf on which various contraceptive devices were displayed, and explained to the red-faced youth what a diaphragm was.

Annoyed by the condescending earnestness of the staff member and the amused glances of those sitting around the table, who seemed to deny the male nurse any semblance of competency for his convictions, simply because he was young and nervous, and enraged as well by the fact that the whole state government would soon be on his back for information with their index cards, state fees, and government doctors, Assen stated nothing but his name and said he didn't want to discuss his reasons for a possible sterilization. The psychologist nodded without looking at him and then got right down to business.

Using an anatomical model, he explained how a vasectomy was performed, its conditions and results, its permanence, the sort of preliminary and follow-up exams that were necessary, and the risks. He emphasized that it was a more or less irreversible procedure, that the section of the vas deferens which was removed could be replaced later by an artificial tube, but that the reestablishment of the spermatic duct would not necessarily result in fertility. From a statistical point of view, that remained more or less a matter of luck. He looked around the circle almost threateningly, and Assen wondered whether he was secretly enjoined by the state to watch over the fertility of its citizens, to protect the continuing presence of the unborn. In reply to the woman's question as to whether the operation affected potency (negatively, she added with a sudden laugh, then covered her mouth), the psychologist shook his head. Sterilization had no effect at all upon the ability to have intercourse. And the common rumors that it affected the hormones, making your voice sound like a woman's, or causing you to start to grow breasts, was all nonsense. Even ejaculation took place as before, for what was normally called sperm in fact contained very few sperm cells. You didn't suddenly have hot air coming out down there.

But, Assen said, if—apart from fertility—no immediate physical or psychological changes are evident, isn't it possible that this little incision will change me in some way that I don't even notice? That my personality will undergo some change when it's divorced from its biological function, some unsuitable change; that I'll still have the same name, the same suits, the same color eyes, but in reality be someone quite different? You see what I mean: the *same* person, developing to a greater or lesser degree in my own eyes and those of my friends—and yet in my heart of hearts empty, a card of the wrong suit, an outcast still trying to play along. Don't I cut myself off from reality with this incision, don't I render myself a phantom, since I destroy any effect I might have, any ongoing effect? Our sex drive is also the pull of the future upon us. Someone who's sterilized feels that as strongly as ever, but can't satisfy it, he's writing checks without any money in the bank. And there'll be no punishment? Think about it: when you're lonely, when you've got no one else to talk to for long periods of time, your perceptions gradually change: you lose the sense of what can be communicated and become duller, even though you consider yourself unchanged, and just as sensitive as ever.

Someone who's been sterilized has been isolated: he can't communicate anymore, his love life, from a biological point of view, retains the mere semblance of communication. Cut off from the unborn, his couplings are fruitless, to put it in high-flown language, he no longer has a role in the future of his race, he is merely present, an idling engine. And how do I know that the loss of this external "physical" dimension might not also result in a spiritual loss over the years, making me more depressed, less imaginative, less articulate, duller, turning me into a man of darkness beneath the same light in which pairs of lovers laugh?

The man in the wheelchair was asleep. The male nurse had stubbed out a small pile of cigarettes. The psychologist shrugged and turned up his hands. —I don't understand what you're getting at, he said. Do you want to be sterilized or not? Assen felt himself turning red with chagrin: he was no longer sure himself. He took a breath for another sentence—but then fell back in his chair and simply waved his hand.

Well it's not really that complicated, said the man with the mustache. Sex after sterilization is still a pleasurable mechanical act, period. And if the operation changes me in some way I don't notice, then it hasn't changed me at all. The rest is splitting hairs on a bald man. If I don't feel well I take a pill, and I feel better again. And if I feel good, I don't give a damn if I'm not well!

Grinning, the psychologist looked at the clock and handed out a few pamphlets as well as lists of doctors who performed vasectomies. —May I say one other thing, the woman said, and pointed to Assen with her stump. Her glasses had slid forward to the tip of her nose, which divided her face at first glance into two halves which didn't quite seem to fit together. If she'd understood him correctly, he just wanted to be a normal person, and yet he was avoiding the most normal thing of all: children. As she'd said, she herself was the mother of four and it certainly hadn't always been easy for her, since she and her husband were both handicapped. Nevertheless—here she turned to the male nurse as well—there was no happiness on earth to compare to having children, raising them with love, and being loved by them in turn. A person who never experienced that had no idea what they were doing to themselves by being sterilized. They didn't know what life was all about. They were just immature. A person like that really shouldn't be . . . What, asked Assen. She looked down. Well, she said, I guess everyone has to decide for themselves.

*

In the subway (he'd left the round table without saying another word) he leafed through the pamphlets and found the psychologist's presentation almost word for word. So the only point of having him appear personally at the health department was to have him register. He cursed the official and tore up the materials.

He declined to try to imagine how the handicapped couple made love. In that family, he thought, there was no room for second thoughts or mental reservations. Instead there must be a caring, carefully calculated exchange, a balanced climate of responsibility in which neither was allowed to be less than was good for the other. One's handicap vitalized the other, in the larger circle of the family each of them was whole, no matter how disabled they were. It was formed and developed in relationship to their disabilities and thereby reduced those disabilities to a tiny melancholy residue. Which of course became intensely painful the moment they left their house and family behind. But the fear of this was simply another reason to band together more strongly, more intimately. While the oldest son tended the wheelchair, tightening a screw here, oiling a hinge there, the younger one trimmed his father's toenails, and the little daughter helped her one-armed mother bake a cake. Holding the wooden rolling pin between them, they rolled out the floury dough.

What would the baby cost him? He could continue living by himself, reading his books, and writing poetry. She would look for an apartment in the neighborhood and he wouldn't see much more of her than he had before. That way the baby would have a father without his being seriously limited in any way. And there were really no financial problems either. He could keep driving the taxi, perhaps an extra day a week, and she, after all, was a student and would receive welfare payments. —Welfare payments? Of course, Iris said, the easiest thing in the world. "Father unknown," that gets you three years on welfare.

He was touched by such a rough-and-ready approach to

life. Arm in arm with the state she was going to foist the joy of a child upon him. When he heard the term "milk allowance" he thought immediately of babies being hushed, of hush money. Suddenly, after all the paving stones hurled down its throat, the Moloch was giving mother's milk. How subversive can you get. But he didn't want to cheat his child's way into the crowd like that. If he was the father, he wanted to be the father, this mayonnaise state wasn't going to father his child: he told her that. She looked up at him from her magazine with a pleased smile, like a mother watching her little boy posing as a muscleman.

*

He already felt himself in the minority. His arguments against having the child were not really arguments, nor were hers on the other side: they were verbal precipitates, poison syringes filled with organic convictions. Because they both knew that Iris would not hesitate to have the child, and that he would not hesitate to abort it, they refused to understand each other. She would have liked to back him up against the wall with her stomach, disarming him with her tender smile, he would have liked to banish her from his world. In fact he threw a book on ecological disasters at her head once, barely missing her. She grabbed him by the hair and pressed up against him, he felt her amazing new body and could only whisper hoarsely.

*

He imagined a murder that left the victim alive and free. To leave and forget might be such a murder, but an imperfect one. The victim would keep popping up in the dreams of the culprit, and over the years destroy him. He recalled a childhood memory, pulling tench from a dredged lake and trying to cut off their heads with a razor. But while he was cutting, his strength and courage kept deserting him; the silence of the gasping fish was a reproach unlike anything he had ever experienced before. At first he wanted to roast them the way they did in all the Indian stories: impale the bodies lengthwise on sticks and hold them over a fire. Now however he thought only of ending their pain, and threw them with their heads half-severed into a fire made out of twigs. He wanted to burn them up completely, to be completely free of his sin. But the flipping bodies beat the flames out. He scraped earth over everything and went away crying.

The next morning a fishtail was sticking out of the leveled sand.

*

A draw. Each of their confrontations ended in a draw that felt to him like defeat. Right or wrong, their opinions were still just opinions, the truth lay elsewhere. Their conversations were judicial sessions dealing with the life and death of a person not present, but Assen felt like he was the accused. Iris left no doubt that she was in the right, she could bear children, so she would bear children. And when she once accused him, among other things, of being jealous of the unborn baby he had to admit it was plausible—but so what? Talking about it seemed more and more absurd to him, laughable: a child conjured up and dismissed with words.

She demanded reasons for his refusal, so he came up with reasons, and sounded to himself as if he were on stage. But he could no more explain his reluctance to have a child than she could explain her desire for one. He was certain about how he felt, but not about how to say it. And Iris confused his doubts about his manner of expression, his hesitant, fumbling attempts at articulation, with indecision, which fired her own eager conviction to the point where at last he tired of opposing the increasing strength of this woman in whom, as he thought, two hearts were already beating.

Listen, she said, when the baby finally arrives, when it's stopped being just an abstraction, you'll like it too. And you'll be ashamed that you reacted to the news of a child as if it were cancer.

*

They met for lunch in a restaurant, drank a lot of wine, and then went to his place. They sat on the carpet, each in a corner of the large room, darkened because of the heat; Assen was smoking. What he could see of Iris, more shadow than form, made him think of a small heap of misery; but there was a sparkle in the region of her eyes. —If looks could kill, she said, took a swallow, put the cork back in the bottle, and shot it over to him like a torpedo. You're emptying my stomach with your silence, you know that. You're bringing me down. What do you take me for, wanting to send me to the slaughterhouse? A house pet, some piece of dirt? — You're drunk, he said, but that's all right. My mother drank a full bottle of cognac when she was seven months pregnant with me. Pardon me, brandy. He took a swallow, corked the bottle, and slid it back in Iris's direction. —Well now, she said, that clears up a few things. She lost her balance reaching for the bottle and tipped over. Her face lay on the carpet, her mouth shoved out of shape; she blinked and stared at him for a long time. One hip was lifted unnaturally high. Do you know what you are? You're not even on the earth anymore, you bookworm. You've cocooned yourself, you're holed up here on your fourth floor. She giggled. And I had to be the one to wander into your stuffy room.

Drunk as he was, he wasn't surprised to see her in the next moment standing before him on unsteady legs. He grabbed her around the waist and tucked her blouse back into her skirt. —Keep your paws off, she said, and sank her fingernails into his shoulders. I still have to bring you into the world, you asshole. A long drop of spittle dribbled from her mouth, she slurped it back. Do you even know what a woman is? You don't want to find out. Your prick's made of paper. You've got typewriter keys for a heart. Why are you wasting your time in this world, tell me that. An antisocial good-for-nothing like you, a pig that eats its own litter. You'd walk over a dead body to keep your life nice and quiet, the peace of the grave, over a dead body!

Her shrill voice filled his ears and he lifted his head, everything spinning. Looking into her red, grimacing face, wet with tears and mucus, he saw through loose strands of hair—illusion or not—the small, hard eyes of his mother, their evil gleam. He simply could not lose himself with love in them. He would be lost. She folded her arms across her chest and wrinkled up her nose, like an animal baring its teeth.

*

A mole had again wandered into the new and still empty
compost pit in their little garden, which had been cemented
in only a few days earlier. Racing about madly, it sought a
way to get back under the earth: the more panicked it
became, the more the knee-deep pit was darkened by the
shadows of children rushing up to see it. It emitted barely
audible squeaks, peeps of distress, and in spite of its tiny size
the play of muscles beneath its gleaming coat seemed powerful. At times it would stop and lift its pink snout toward
those standing above, who strained to find its invisible eyes,
or clapped their hands with delight. Then it would start
running again with a strange undulating, waddling gait, a
tiny circus bear. The shape and color of its paws, turned far
out from its body, reminded little Assen of the soft hands of
his Punch and Judy dolls. —An antisocial individualist, said
one of the older boys, as if he were reading from a textbook.
He told them what he knew: that moles lived only four or
five years, not because that was long enough and they were
tired of life, but because their tiny teeth wore down, worn
away by the sandy food they ate, worms mostly. They
couldn't eat anything else, so they starved to death. Their
eyes are no bigger than the poppy seeds on a bread roll,
they're concealed behind folds of skin and come out when
they're needed. They're not blind, as people often think. On
the contrary, they can distinguish between light and dark as
can almost all living creatures, and they even have a lens in
their eye that scientists have found no explanation for,
whose complicated structure lets them see things that are
invisible to us. —The spirit-world, Assen murmured to
himself in fascination, and listened as the boy went on to say

that any animal—be it snake, mouse, or even one of its own kind—that accidentally entered a mole's burrow was as good as dead.

Suddenly he felt a sharp nudge. His mother told him to fetch a shovel. —The coal shovel, she called after him. It had a large, flat scoop and a curved grip on the handle. When he returned with it, the other children looked at him like he was going to spoil their fun. His mother pushed them aside. Following her instructions, he placed the scoop flat on the bottom of the pit and then jerked it up quickly just as the mole was running across it. It was funny the way it flew straight up through the air with its front paws out side-ways—as if its thumbs were stuck comfortably behind its suspenders. It landed softly on a pile of freshly turned garden soil and had already disappeared a third of the way in with a few powerful crawling motions when Assen's mother screamed *Kill it!*

She screamed it repeatedly, in such quick succession that the words were transformed in a centrifuge of rage and disgust into howling tears that mounted to hysterical cries more quickly than the animal could dig into the earth— accompanied by the frantic clicking of her wooden heels as she stamped her feet in a frenzy. Assen turned quickly to look at her, and then at the children, from whom he could see he would get no help, and thought of running away. But looking into his mother's bright red, distorted face, into her punishing eyes, he saw for one terrible moment his own features, tear-stained and twisted in pain beneath her blows—and in his sad confusion he simply let the heavy shovel fall on the spot where nothing was now visible but the short, bristly tail of the mole. And there it stayed. One of the children drew a whistling breath through his teeth, all their faces turned toward him, and he let the handle slip from his moistened hands. He'd killed it. —Thank god, his mother said, it would have ruined the whole garden.

*

In the neighboring apartment on the same floor, in the connecting wing of the building which was still occupied, the doors banged so loudly that the thin inner wall trembled. One of those seal-fat Berlin bass voices sounded through the rooms, a shrill woman's voice replied, Assen could understand individual words, whisky glass, filthy pig, bullshit. The woman's nagging and screaming rose higher and higher, as if her larynx were about to jump into her mouth, the man's braying in the meantime soon faded to an insulted mumble and finally died away altogether. For a while all was still. Suddenly the man let out a triumphant growl and something that made Assen think immediately of coal briquettes rattled to the wood floor. —One, the man roared, and two, apparently throwing a handful of briquettes through the apartment each time. The woman's soaring screams, the hair-raising insults, suddenly turned into a deep sobbing. And three. Assen pictured her cowering at the end of the long hall, eyeing her husband through the well-groomed hands she holds over her face. —That's the worst thing, he heard him bellow: I always get hot again. Everything would be all right if I didn't get hot again! Something scraped against the wall, glass shattered, and coals were sent rolling, as if they had been swept aside by the man as he crawled toward his wife. A mumbling reconciliation. Quiet. Assen imagined how his dirty hand swept over her face, across her closed eyes, over her pouting lower lip, coming to rest on her breast. In his vision the breast was amputated, the bodice a collapsing hill.

*

Women, said Lauter, are a means of locomotion; they have the direction in mind, all we provide is the gas. They pull us out from behind the page and career with us through their life histories until we think they're ours, until our own past seems as strange and distant as some out of the way rest stop on the Autobahn. They sit on our egos so often we can't say "I" anymore. And when we tell them to back off a bit and let us alone for a while, they spin the steering wheel, we're thrown out and wake up in the ditch with our heads busted. I haven't met one yet who deep down inside didn't want to have it *all*, even if it turned out to be worse than nothing in the cold light of day: a husband, kids, the whole kit and kaboodle. And as long as women exist, no crazy feminist ideas can ever change that. They want a family so bad that they change the wildest orgy into a middle-class marriage, the hottest fights into a lazy peace. You want to alter your relationship—she alters an evening dress. You want to set the world on fire—she bakes a cake. You grab her by the throat—she turns her eyes imploringly toward the kid. When you think you've got her in the palm of your hand, she puts the squeeze on you; first you're stuck on her, then you're stuck with her. So what if I'll never figure 'em out? What gets me is that they'll never figure themselves out either. What can I say? They live so unconsciously they don't even realize it. They think with their smell, they write poetry with their hips. A guy like me can only stand there like an idiot in the tin suit of my character and let them pass by like a thunderstorm.

An old guy I know who doesn't write a line anymore except on his tab said something interesting recently: You're a Don Juan, he said, just like in the book. But the sad thing is that the sort of women you're looking for don't exist anymore, these days they're all flat on their backs before you can finish your drink. And there you sit with nothing to crow about: seduction's no big deal anymore. A Don Juan these days is as pathetic as a farmer in a spaceship. You're an anachronism, a bull that keeps charging a red polyester cape and never realizes he's attacking himself, just goring himself. You think you're seducing someone and instead she's leading you around by the nose with a golden ring. A Don Juan doesn't need his strength and energy to find a woman and get her in bed these days, he needs it to keep her off his back.

The old bastard's right. Of course I know I'm oversimplifying things when I say that women are the enemy. In some sense we represent a unity in the larger divine order of things; each of us the other side of the coin, even if the coin is counterfeit. But that's a little too cozy for me. I need their resistance, need those sweet tongues to test my bitter principles—just as I need my neuroses and traumas, need to struggle with them, if I want to stay halfway healthy and alive. "Gender tension," some sociologist called it recently, a good customer, and when I asked him if he was talking about electricity, he ordered only seltzer water from then on. Why admit that my gut reaction to these soul monsters is fear? They'd ram me cap-first into the soil like a stone dwarf in a garden. So I suck in my belly and give my voice that deep wolfish sound that gives them goose bumps and fills my featherbed. They don't realize I can't give them what they want until the next morning. What do they expect? Devotion? The word's a boot heel on my neck.

*

Softly, as if a breeze had turned in the lock, the apartment door opened, then shut again immediately. Assen heard the landlord running down the stairs, grabbed a coat hanger from the wardrobe, and was about to set out after him when the telephone rang.

All right then, Iris said without a word of greeting: things can't go on this way. I for one am tired of always thinking of new points. All this talk is making me sick. It's not my job to make you grow up. Apparently you don't love me enough to have this child with me; what else am I supposed to think about your constant stubbornness, your empty defiance. On the other hand—she lit a match and inhaled the cigarette smoke loudly—on the other hand I apparently don't love you enough to give it up for you. I'm going to have it without you and your support, let me finish. You don't have to worry, it won't cost you anything, you'll be just as free as ever. I'm sending you a notarized statement in which I take over full custody of our baby and release you from all duties and any type of responsibility, for life. If I should die or have a fatal accident, my sister will take over the child's care and education. That'll be notarized too and should meet with your approval. Other than that: good-bye.

"The delivery," Assen said to himself, and heard in the sudden stillness the distant sounds of other people talking on the line, joking indistinctly.

You can't do that, he said softly, almost whispering, then repeated it quickly, shouting. He stood at the window, punched the cardboard from the frame of the broken window, sunlight poured into the room like a rafter in which dust swirled lazily. Down in the courtyard the landlord was standing on a pile of construction sand; he stuck out his tongue at Assen, jerking his empty hand back and forth quickly in front of his fly. Iris was silent for a few moments before she hung up; it had a cautious sound, as if she'd depressed the receiver with her little finger.

*

He called her several times after that without reaching her. The entire commune seemed to be covering for her—at any rate he couldn't imagine that she was going on with life as usual and just happened to always be in study groups or seminars, or at the restaurant or the movies. He went to the post office to send a telegram. When the woman asked him what he wanted to say, he looked at her for a long time blankly, without seeing her. Then he turned around abruptly and walked out. But five minutes later he returned to the window. No words, he said, just a question mark. The woman lowered her head and looked at him over the invisible rim of her glasses. A question mark is not a word, young man, I can only send words with syllables. A question mark, he said, I want to send a question mark. She lifted her chin. Next, please. Question mark, Assen said, write: question mark stop.

*

When they finally told him that Iris had gone to Italy for a few months he shouted "Liar" into the phone, ran out of the building, and took a taxi to her place. A woman he'd never seen before opened the door, but she evidently knew who he was. She nodded wordlessly toward one of the closed doors. At first the only way he knew that the room behind the door belonged to Iris was by the photos that showed her with her sister's baby. In the wide-open empty wardrobe a single hanger dangled, swaying as if the coat had just been removed from it. A chair stood on the desk. The carpet was rolled up against the wall. The furniture was covered with sheets. Assen pulled open a drawer; two green lemons rolled about inside.

After the meal he ordered a small pot of coffee and shredded the blood-red paper napkin. The streetlights were just coming on. Two policemen took carry-out food to their car and drove away, leaving the view clear to the white-tiled café across the way. The counter behind the front window was a close-knit construction of neon tubes whose

strong glow turned the clothes of those standing at it translucent; their movements trembled in the neon lights as if
captured with a hand-held camera. Scattered customers sat
at black enameled tables, their cheeks dimpling into shadow
as they sucked at their straws. Four young American soldiers in civilian clothes, wearing German air force flight
jackets, crowded in front of the jukebox, their faces bathed
in blue light, choosing old rock-and-roll tunes that echoed
across the street, banging at the buttons with their beer
glasses, half dancing, half wrestling. One of them discovered the hidden switch, turned up the volume, and looked
around defiantly at the other customers, who glanced up or
gave a start, but seemed to take no further notice.

A glassful of beer sprayed through the smoke, and the
four men began to dance more aggressively, stamping their
heels and jerking their shoulders, as if they were barging
into the air around them. In the face of their ungainly and
obscene movements, several of the customers withdrew into
the interior of the bar, without interrupting their conversations. But the eagerness with which they spoke to one another now seemed forced; they stared into each other's eyes
as if they were mouse holes offering refuge. Love me tender, Assen heard, while the first glass shattered on the tile
floor, one soldier kicked smoking holes in the neon along
the counter, and another knocked the phone from the hand
of a waitress, a fragile looking blond with bright-red lipstick,
ripping it off the cord. Assen poured himself a cup of coffee
with a motion that caused it to slop back up over the edge.

Now one of the Americans was going around the tables
holding his hand out open to the customers, who either

blushed or turned pale. Each of them hastened to give him a few coins—except for one woman, who indicated she didn't have any more money. He picked up her wine glass and emptied it with one swallow, then hurled it against the front window, where it shattered. The soldiers counted the money, hooting, and the one who'd collected it put a few coins in the jukebox. Then he took up a position near the customers who were crowding anxiously around the pinball machine. His hands on his hips, he thrust out his chin and yelling something unintelligible, stamped his heels, and growled, as if he were trying to provoke a dog. Then with a curse he hurled the rest of the change at them, and Assen watched as the coins rained against raised arms, eyeglasses, and bared teeth.

A young, long-haired man in brightly colored patched jeans entered the café. Fumbling at the ties of his windbreaker, he went directly to the bar and ordered. It wasn't until the woman at the bar failed to react, continuing instead to stare straight in front of her with her arms folded defiantly on her chest, that he noticed the broken glass everywhere, the kicked-in bar, and the Americans, who cocked their heads at him. He turned back to the woman, who now said something to him out of the corner of her mouth while she lit a cigarette. He hunched his shoulders slightly and slowly turned around. At his first step toward the door, one of the soldiers spat a piece of gum into his hair, and at the second step another tossed a full glass of beer at his feet. The man went rigid. But after a glance at the other customers, who had started talking again as if they hadn't seen anything, he gave a start, stepped up to the Americans, and began talking to them, his face flushed, his hands turned outward in protest.

They listened a while, their heads lowered threateningly, or raised high, then jostled each other and began laughing. The young man, obviously relieved, was also smiling now. One soldier punched him good-naturedly on the shoulder, another held out his hand. But as he reached for it, the man pulled it back quickly and gestured behind him with his thumb. He grabbed the man by the collar and dragged him out of the bar. The others blocked the door.

On the sidewalk he shoved him forward, as if he were giving him a head start. The man threw his hair back and pushed a strand behind his ear, his eyes were invisible behind the blank glaze of his glasses. He had full, almost feminine lips. The first blow turned him half way around, his arms flew out like a doll. He brought both hands to his mouth, and as he looked in shock at his blood-covered fingers the second blow caught him, knocking his glasses to the ground, smashing them: a broken rim bounced off the window where Assen was sitting, a car ran over what remained of the frames. The man stumbled two steps forward toward his attacker and fell to his knees. He held his hands over his face. The blood flowed down to the sidewalk in long drops through his fingers.

Assen grabbed the arms of his chair to get up, but could only clutch them. Sweat broke out on his upper lip, his heart was hammering, as if it were idling at a high rate of speed. He wanted to be paralyzed by shock, but he only felt limp with fear. He wished desperately that what was happening outside would happen faster, so fast he couldn't react to it.

(Later he was surprised that he never for a moment thought of the police.) He looked around; men were sitting at tables behind him, eating. They were looking out the window, but none of them seemed to see anything. And in the café across the way, behind the Americans, beer was again being served.

The man who had been hit, still on his knees, was swaying back and forth. Behind his hands a dark, gurgling sobbing was audible, muffled by the window and sounding even more terrible because of it. The soldier, whose jaw was working brightly in his darkened face, circled the moaning man. His relaxed manner was reminiscent of a world-class soccer player placing the ball for a penalty shot. As the beaten man let his hands fall and looked up imploringly, the American took one step backward, his arms extended, his fists clenched. Then, staring blankly above his victim, he kicked him. The man threw his arms in the air, his mouth gaping. Blood shot from his nose over his teeth, bared in a spasm of unimaginable pain. He keeled over and lay motionless. Calling out something to the others, the soldier kicked him again in the head, which now jerked loosely from one shoulder to the other. His friends rushed out the door and pulled him away. A strong breeze had come up, their flight jackets billowed in the wind as they disappeared down the next side street.

Assen paid. When the waitress walked away, he stuck a steak knife in his jacket and left the bar. From every direction came the sound of flapping, snapping awnings, car antennas swayed in the blustery wind, sudden gusts blew flower pots off the balconies into brightly lit apartments.

Surrounded by customers from the café, the wounded man sat on the curb holding his head in both hands. Two women were consoling him, dabbing his face with white paper napkins, a third held bandages in readiness. He looked up as Assen walked by; a quiet, alert look, somehow strengthened, an almost thoughtful indignation. A man brought him a whiskey, while another gestured angrily in the direction the soldiers had taken.

Assen turned into the side street, which was dark and empty except for the neon sign outside a wine cellar, a rooster in red glass with the head knocked off. It started to rain, rustling in the tops of the chestnut trees, drumming on car tops, the water ran down the back of his hands and wet his cigarette, which fell apart between his fingers. He stopped and stared along the dark sidewalk into the tangle of falling rain and the bright spray of rebounding droplets. He felt the hatred grow within him, yet realized he was secretly exaggerating it to hold on to the clarity of the feeling. There seemed to him no point in considering these men as individuals, as if they had committed a crime. They *were* the crime—but it was probably this thought too, and the fear that after his cowardice he would be too weak to take strong action, that drove him onward. Torn within, he now wished only to kill.

At first he didn't see the soldiers on the four-lane Kleistsstrasse. The streetlights flowed across his glasses with the water, he wiped them off with his bare hand. He heard glass break beneath the arch of the elevated railway that led, dimly illuminated, toward the center of the city, then an echoing laugh, and he raced across the street. Under the overpass, already nearing the end of the steel construction, the Americans were shuffling along. Their footsteps echoed as if they were behind him. One of them struck a girder with something made of iron, and the bright sound set his teeth on edge. Fresh drops of blood shimmered on the pavement, the American must have cut his fist on the man's glasses. Assen tried to walk as quietly as possible, gripped the handle of the knife in his jacket pocket, and took long strides, almost skipping, barely touching the ground. Gusts of rain blew in under the overpass from both sides.

As the Americans turned into Potsdamer Strasse he started to run, his tie fluttering over his shoulder. He was sweating in the rain, his glasses loosened and danced up and down on the bridge of his nose. He was breathing through clenched teeth, blowing tiny bubbles of saliva. His shadow lengthened before him and flitted to the side in the rhythm of the lampposts. It was as if he were chasing his anger, which was becoming weaker and weaker, more and more threadbare, and he felt he might just as well stop running and walk away in some other direction. So he ran even faster, change rattling in his pockets, the speed driving out all thought, and his rage returned. He drifted wide rounding a corner, as if he were on a stadium track, and sliding to a stop before an advertisement pillar, he almost ran right into the soldiers.

They were leaning at the counter of a snack bar, pulling the tabs from large golden beer cans. He gripped the knife more tightly, as if it were a gearshift going into reverse, and stumbled back two steps over his own feet. The blade ripped through his jacket pocket and gleamed in the neon light—

but the four men, who now had their heads together over the flame of a cigarette lighter, paid no attention. Only one of them glanced up at him, through him, his beer can smeared with blood. Assen pretended to be drunk, stumbled on a few meters, and waited in the entranceway to a building.

A cigarette later they crossed the street in the direction of Kreuzberg, their jackets pulled over their heads. The shadow of the little group brushed gigantically along a gabled wall, the lighter part of the bottoms of their boots, where the sole curved inward, gleamed as they walked in step. A prostitute stepped out of a gateway toward them and then immediately retreated. Somewhere in the dark a window closed, the panes rattling. A cat slipped under a car, its eyes glowed greenly in the dark, then turned amber with a blink. Steam rose from a ventilation shaft. The Americans turned into a small park in which a single tall streetlamp was burning, wrapped in a rainy mist. They suddenly stopped. They took their hands from their pockets, one of them looked around quickly. Assen stepped back into the shadow of a tree.

On the green meadow, between tipped-over or broken benches (at first he'd thought what he saw was a small rise in the ground) lay a woman. She was lying prone, her arms outspread, as if she'd been run over. She was wearing a calf-length black raincoat, soaking wet strands of hair covered her face. Near her right hand, on which a few rings gleamed, stood a purse. One of the soldiers yelled something that Assen couldn't understand, approached her slowly, stretched his foot out, and poked the woman with the tip of his shoe. She didn't stir; even when he wiped the hair out of her face and blew cigarette smoke in her unfocused eyes. While he picked up the purse and rummaged through it, then dropped it again, he must have made a joke, because the others broke out in loud laughter. Then—his friends were already walking on—he pissed in it. Assen shut his eyes for a moment. Beneath the thick, steaming stream of the swaying man he heard small bottles and tubes click against one another.

Now! he hissed, and stepped out from behind the tree. He was surprised to find that he felt neither excitement nor fear. Four or five steps separated him from his victim, who was already in his shadow, his eyes opened wide. The man's surprise gave Assen strength and courage, growling with satisfaction he reached in his pocket and focused upon the other's throat, on which he saw a small tattoo, a flower. His teeth clenched, his shoulders hunched, his muscles rigid to the point of pain, he felt as if he had stepped into an electric field. A shiver ran over his scalp and raised his hair on end, a sudden rush of heat fogged his glasses. He stuck his fingers through the hole he'd made in his pocket, and found himself facing the soldier empty-handed. The knife had disappeared.

Still pissing, the American lifted his chin. He probably took him for a drunk or a bum, at any rate he didn't seem disturbed, if anything he appeared to follow with interest the way Assen started patting himself all over in shock, more and more quickly, as if he were looking for his keys or a missing theater ticket, while he twisted the jacket around his body and retreated step by step. The soldier buttoned his fly, put his hands on his hips, and watched him silently a while longer. Finally he spat out his gum and walked calmly after his friends.

*

Assen began to shiver. He stepped back into the shadow of the tree and felt around on the ground, searching in vain for his knife among the corks, cigarette butts, and broken bottles. He stuck his hand through the hole in his jacket again and again, grabbing his own fingers in disbelief when they poked through. He scraped through the grass with his shoe, even turning over a few clods and scattered bits of paper, then peered at the sidewalk, when the woman at his feet coughed. It was a strained and painful cough, louder and louder, as if forced through her body from the earth's interior, until it shook her entire frame, followed by a thick surge of vomit, and Assen, as he watched the soldiers disappearing between the rows of houses, compressed his lips above his cramped and trembling chin, cried, yet in the rain could feel no tears, and knelt down beside her.